DO
BA

DOCTOR WHO

BATTLEFIELD

Based on the BBC television series by Ben Aaronovitch
by arrangement with BBC Books, a division of BBC
Enterprises Ltd

MARC PLATT

Number 152 in the
Target Doctor Who Library

TARGET

Published in 1991
By Target Books
an imprint of Virgin Publishing Ltd
338 Ladbroke Grove
London W10 5AH

The BBC producer of *Battlefield* was John Nathan-Turner
The director was Michael Kerrigan
The role of the Doctor was played by Sylvester McCoy

Typeset by Type Out, London SW16
Printed and bound in Great Britain by
Cox & Wyman Ltd, Reading

ISBN 0 426 20350 X

For Ben
the perfect gentle Knight who let
his humble squire take over the reins

PROLOGUE

Three sisters bore him down to the boat. Swan-haired and regal, each was crowned with a circlet of silver and robed in weeds of darkest green. Sisters, yet each also a queen from one of the Thirteen Planets. Summoned, even in the final throes of war, to another Universe as the prophecy decreed. Two queens to carry the High King. One queen to tend his wounds.

The aged king was armoured in black with the crest of the Pendragon on his breastplate. Lying still on the pallet, he gazed up into the endless blue of the sky over Avallion. He searched for the corridor gate that led back to the home dimension, but he could no longer focus on the invisible as Merlin had once shown him.

With the bulk of his army scattered, this final battle had become a rout. He had been trying to rally his forces, any forces at all, when out of the smoke came three of Morgaine's rabble. Three grey knights from her personal entourage, fiercely trained and with the arrogance of near victory in their gait.

They had circled round him, just out of reach, neither attacking nor parrying, but they laughed mockingly at their lucky catch.

He knew they were confining him in a cage until Mordred might arrive to take the glory as the High King's executioner. Where was the honour in that? But what did Mordred have to do with honour? There was no honour even in Mordred's

1

conceiving.

'Excalibur,' he had warned the grey knights, lifting the fabled blade for them to recognize. Together, he and the weapon were one; sword and swordsman understood one another and were terrible in the havoc they could wreak. But the knights only backed off a little.

Instead he had made to run, but only to draw the knights back in on him.

Three against one. Excalibur leapt eagerly out and slew the first two with one swing that nearly carried the king's arm from its socket.

The third knight ducked and brought his sword in low. The blow caught the king on the right knee, slicing into the hydraulic muscle of his armour's joint. The old warrior pitched forward in the mud, but his jewelled sword swung itself back and took off the knight's arm.

As the king lay alone and cold, trying to gather his fleeting senses, he had heard the knight weeping in pain. Then there was quiet. No birds sang near the battle. The yells and screams of the fighting had grown more distant.

Close at hand, a sudden voice whispered, 'My lord king.'

He opened his eyes and saw Bedivere bending over him. The young black-armoured knight was helmless. He was pale and there was a crimson gash across his forehead.

'Water,' said the king. He tried to raise himself, but his armour was lifeless and he could not manage the effort alone. He felt Bedivere lift him easily in his arms and start to carry him. He swooned.

He was weary of fighting. Full weary of the hatred that beset the world like a plague. And weary of Morgaine's endless plans to assert her dark order on them all. A weary and old king.

She worked ceaselessly to overthrow him with her black arts. Everything around him was crumbling. Everything he knew and loved was either smashed or stolen. Most of all, he was weary of having to make decisions alone where Merlin once would advise him. But he would never cease to resist her monstrous duplicity.

He had smelt the lake before he saw it. The lake on whose

2

banks the Pendragon had once defeated Vortigern the Usurper. On the Isle of Apples, away from the world, the willows were burgeoning into new leaf. Avallion in springtime. Yellow flags grew among the rushes at the waterside. He saw them fluttering like battle standards as the three women settled him on to a pallet constructed from linen and spear shafts. The prophecy was familiar, but the outcome either eluded him or he refused to remember.

Bedivere stood watching nearby, his handsome head bowed to hide his tears. Beyond him, along the bank, a group of local peasants stared, uncomprehending, by their rough huts of wattle.

Now the women were loading the king into the boat. His chest was tight and wet inside the dead armour and he began to cough, feeling a trickle run down through his beard. He moved his hand against his side and shuddered.

'My sword! Excalibur!' Surely it could not have left him now? 'Excalibur!' Why did they not listen? Merlin would have listened.

Queen Selysette of Lyonce leaned in over him to wipe away the blood.

'My sword! I must have it! And the scabbard!'

She nodded gravely to Bedivere who had drawn closer on the bank. The king heard his faithful young knight pounding away into the distance.

'It will come,' said the queen.

Mist drifted across the sky overhead. Or was it smoke from the battle? A full minute passed before the king realized that the boat was moving away from the shore. But the queen had given her word. The sword would come.

The gentle rhythmic swish of the boat's fins as it paddled over the lake eased his mind. The mist closed in and the king scarcely noticed as a shimmering dome rose like a bubble around the boat's occupants. It sank slowly beneath the surface of the lake and the light around it deepened into a water-dappled green.

It seemed to the king that he was sinking down a great well. And then the well became a tall tower with walls of water lifting high above him. They glittered and streamed with rising columns of tiny bubbles. He began to be afraid. He dared not move or breathe for fear that one tiny disturbance would bring the walls cascading down upon him in a torrential flood of retribution.

This was a trap. Some hateful witchery of Morgaine's devising, like that with which she, in the guise of Nimue, had thought to entomb Merlin in the ice forest beneath Breceliande. Yet while the king lived, all those days of chivalry were not dead. He could rebuild his world again. He had fought alone against worse odds than this and battled worse monsters. And everything that Merlin had taught him as a boy, everything the aged wizard and counsellor complained that he had forgotten, was coming back to him. Clear and fresh as the air after a storm. The son of the Pendragon would return. It had been foretold. He could fight alone again.

The high walls of water above him teetered in and blocked the light. Plunged into darkness he cried out again for his sword.

A new but dim light appeared from the side. The king managed to raise himself, but the pallet on which he lay lurched as the queens lifted it from the dry-docked boat. He watched the light approach as they neared its source, until they finally emerged into a wide and familiar hall. The dark glossy walls rose high into the gloom. He could make out arrays of heraldic devices along the consoles that lined the wide floor. The solemn tranquillity of the place was almost tangible. It had been genetically designed to be so. It should have been like coming home.

A single shaft of light fell from the roof and illuminated a black slab of obsidian like an altar at the centre of the hall. There was a figure standing in front of the slab, silhouetted against the light. As the king's cortege crossed the floor, their footsteps echoing back at them, the figure stretched out its arms in greeting and stepped backwards into the pool of light.

The king caught his breath in disbelief. 'Merlin! Against all hope…'

The wizard smiled impishly at his aged royal pupil. 'I see you've been killing people again, Arthur. Another fine pickle you've got yourself into!'

The armour ran faster than Bedivere's legs could carry him.

His own muscles ached to tearing point as he almost fell down the bank towards the willows and skidded to a halt at the water's edge. The boat was gone.

Staring out across the lake, he thought he glimpsed the featureless shape of the boat disappearing into the mist. He clutched his king's sacred sword and its scabbard in his fists.

What could he do now? How could he return Excalibur? At all costs the sword must be kept from the enemy. But there were no allies to turn to. No prisoners were being taken. All captives were being put to the sword by the victors on Mordred's orders.

Avallion was a prison. His helm had been shattered in the battle and he could not leap through infinity to his own dimension without it. He was trapped in a cold and barbaric reality, a universe away from home and love. But he must forget his honour and hide himself, living on his wits until his mission was fulfilled. That was nothing. Galahad had endured far worse for the Grail.

He looked out over the lake again. The mist had suddenly cleared to reveal the far bank, but there was no sign of the boat.

He heard the clank of armour and saw a group of grey knights running along the bank towards him. There were more coming from the other direction. He had nowhere to run to, but they would not have Excalibur.

Flinging aside the scabbard, he began to wade out into the water. The knights began to splash in after him, swords raised.

Powering up the tension of the hydraulic muscle in his right side armour, he lifted Excalibur high behind him. With a yell, he pitched the sword as far out over the water as the armour would throw it. He felt a fierce stab of pain as his arm fractured, and then he was dragged back by force and found a sword at his throat.

Excalibur gleamed in the sunlight as it began to fall over the centre of the lake. Before it struck the surface, there was a flash of white and the sword vanished as if it had been snatched away by a burning fist of fire.

The arm around Bedivere's throat wrenched back in anger. The other knights were forming a circle around him in the water.

'Where's Arthur?' yelled the voice at his ear. Bedivere knew

5

the voice only too well and loathed it with all his heart.

'Safe away from you, Mordred Fitzroy! King's bastard!'

There were no more questions to ask. And nothing that Bedivere would answer. Staring up at the sky towards home, he hardly felt the sword that cut into his throat.

'A once and future king?' complained Merlin. 'Dear oh dear, I thought we'd given up all that nonsense.' He shook his head of unruly red hair in irritation. 'Isn't enough ever enough?'

Arthur raised himself painfully from the side of the chair where they had sat him. He slammed his gloved fist against the carved arm. 'You gave your word!'

'I most certainly did not! You've been listening to those minstrels again. They always exaggerate.'

'Teeth of Heaven!' A series of coughs tore up from Arthur's aching lungs. He pushed away the queen who moved in to tend him and wiped the fresh blood from his mouth himself. 'You are never here when I have need of you, Merlin.'

The wizard shrugged and smiled weakly, revealing the laughter lines on his avuncular face. 'I can't be everywhere at once.'

But there was still mischief behind his eyes. And he still looked younger every time he returned.

Arthur rested his head back on the side of the chair. He looked around the dark ribs of the King's Hall ship that Merlin had cultured for him long, long ago in the vat-cellars of the High Tagel. The consoles bleeped quietly as they awaited his instructions. Always ready to jump the stars or outfly the swiftest ornithopter.

'Ten years of war have we suffered. My wife and friend are lost to me. The alliance of the Round Table is broken. My kingdom is slipping away. The land dies.'

'Morgaine has grown in power.'

'She will destroy us all with her black arts.'

'I doubt that, Arthur. But it may be a long struggle.'

'I thought I had lost my tutor too. And then you return against all odds, but only to snatch away my remaining hope.'

'Oh, don't be so gloomy. And never trust people who make

prophesies.'

Arthur lifted his eyes in disbelief. 'But you do naught else!'

'It's one of my more annoying habits.'

The High King of the Thirteen Worlds gripped the arms of the chair and struggled to rise. He cursed as his knees buckled under him. The dead armour was cumbersome and he was too weak to move against it. He sat back temporarily defeated. But he would find a way.

He missed Lancelot. And he longed to see Guenever again and ask for her forgiveness.

Merlin took a salve-sponge from one of the queens and began gently to wipe the mud and blood from the aged king's face.

'My dear Arthur, I think it's time I came clean with you.'

'Excalibur,' he muttered. 'Where is it?'

'You see it's all very well calling me tutor, but I can't even begin your education until I find out how all this ends.'

To Merlin's surprise, the king appeared to rally from his misery. 'So it is true then,' he said eagerly.

'True? Why? What else have the minstrels been saying?'

'That you live your life backwards.'

'No, no, no!'

From his tatty embroidered Afghan coat, Merlin tugged a floppy hat of brown felt. He flailed it into shape as he tried to contain his annoyance. Around its brim, the saffron Katmandu bandana was creased and tangled. A pair of finger cymbals tinkled to the floor. 'My life may be rather haphazard — in a temporal sort of way. But I cannot predict the future...'

'You deny it yet again!'

'Of course I do! And you know that.'

'So you cannot say the hour of my death.'

The wizard smiled inwardly that the old king could still beat his tutor into a corner. He looked forward to beginning the young king's education. But there seemed no way to convince his old friend that time was passing. All things had their time and that included the time to let go of what you loved.

'I shall rise again,' continued Arthur. 'There is no question. I decree it. And I shall see Morgaine defeated. And you, Merlin, I rely on to see me win through!'

7

Merlin's twin hearts sank. 'I'll see what I can do, my lord,' he said quietly. 'It may already be in hand.'

The king grunted. Satisfied at last, he leaned back into his chair. 'And find my sword too.'

There was a movement in the shadows at the back of the hall. One of the queens, Bellangere of Orlamande, lifted Excalibur from the cavity into which it had been peristalted by the ship. She carried the ancient sword with reverence to Merlin.

'But there is no scabbard,' she said.

'I'm sure it'll turn up again some time.' Merlin held the sword for a moment, recognizing the filigree ganglia systems worked out in the hilt and the blade.

'I am hight Escalibore,
Unto a king fair tresore.'

'Thank you, your majesties,' he said gravely. 'Your part in this will be remembered.'

The three attendant queens bowed low to him. Then he turned to present the sword to its true master.

The king was already sleeping. A new serenity drained the aching weariness from his face. His breathing steadied.

The queens watched Merlin carry the sword, symbol of the High Kingship, to the central control console. He found the key input socket that he had grafted into the obsidian unit, because he remembered that long ago he had found it there in the future. He slowly, ceremonially, lowered the blade into its place.

'So my once and future friend, the Night Watch begins.'

The huge amethyst in the hilt glittered momentarily with fire. The gentle hum of the ship pitched up a degree.

High King Arthur shifted in his sleep. 'Thank you, Doctor,' he muttered through his dreams.

Part 1

Scenario: Dull Swords

'Alle be ware
Of they that stare.
Theyre watchful minde
Behind theyre eyes
Already blinde
From stareful glare.'

The Watchers Songe
Anonymous 29th Century Bardic Ballad

Chapter 1

They pulled Bambera out of the Zambezi valley days from Koroi. An army surplus Hind-24 gunship picked her up and flew her back to Harare. The controls were still labelled in Cyrillic lettering and the Chinese-trained pilot cursed in Shona all the way to the airport.

A first class seat on the Swissair flight to Geneva. Her weapons as hand luggage in a diplomatic bag above her head. German businessmen furtively studied her over folded copies of *Der Spiegel* and the *Wall Street Journal*. She accepted the compliments of the airline, picked at the *poule à la reine* with a plastic fork, and drank herself stupid.

She woke up in the Geneva BOQ, tangled in crisp and damp cotton. She was still holding the whisky bottle; its label was Japanese. Stumbling into the bathroom, she dropped it into the rubbish bin. There were echoes of a nightmare in her head, but the details were gone.

She stared into the mirror over the sculpted plastic basin, daring herself to throw up.

A shower helped. She looked down at her feet and saw the water stained mud brown as it swirled away. Fifteen days in the Zambezi valley washing down the drain. She wrapped herself in the soft laundered towels and sat looking at the trouser press and the kettle. She would have to force down some coffee. One cup made with two individual sachets. No milk.

UNIT passports are never stamped by customs. No questions asked, no nationality given. The pages stay pristine, only the magnetic strip on the back changes. Bambera's military career reduced to ghost lines in iron oxide, to muddy sheets in nameless rooms, ribbons in storage.

A dress uniform hung on the wardrobe door, a tiny store of cocoa butter on the dresser. Next to it, by the coffee sachets, a white plastic afro comb in a sterile wrapping.

Bambera sat with her back to the mirror and combed her hair.

Orders were waiting in gold and silicon, wrapped in matt black plastic. Bambera slapped the EPROM cartridge into her portable file, keyed in her security code and dumped it into memory. She read the information as it scrolled up on the small LCD screen.

Dull Sword, she thought, a non-significant incident involving a nuclear weapon.

Salamander Six-Zero, a ground-launched cruise missile system, in breach of the Berlin Convention.

Not many left now, but their disposal had to be discreet. One at a time. Bambera's turn had come round again.

She could feel a dull pain building up above her left eye. The soft burr of the air-conditioning nagged at her head, far worse than the stridulant insect life of the Zambezi. There had been a time when she never got a hangover. There had been a time when she never had time to drink properly at all.

Why do they always give these jobs to me?

UNIT HQ was an old finishing school perched over the lake six klicks from Geneva. In her imagination, the girls were always white and insubstantial as wraiths. Clustering in the polished hallways, heads dipped towards each other as they exchanged confidences. Learning how to dance and curtsey in the large, high ceilinged rooms, before running like so many Isadora Duncans out on to the lawns to vanish in the sunlight.

The BOQ was a wooden annexe built in chalet style to the north of the main building. Bambera walked across the damp lawn. To her left a hydrofoil was cutting a white wake across the steel grey lake. The mountains beyond were shadows in the overcast sky.

11

She flipped her card at one of the Swiss guards in her glass box by the side entrance. The guard unsealed the door and she stepped inside. Both passenger lifts were out of order, so Bambera went down in the service elevator with half a tonne of electronics and a new coffee machine.

Two hundred metres down, the doors opened on to a long corridor with puff concrete walls. Black electrical cables spewed out of the ceiling and snaked across the floor. The air smelt of damp cement.

A young private snapped to attention as Bambera stepped from the lift. The private was young with wide Slavic features and small, close-set eyes; one of the new intake recruited directly by the United Nations. For a horrible moment, Bambera thought from the look of recognition that the girl was going to ask for her autograph. But she saluted instead. Bambera returned the salute with more crispness than usual; she'd been young once.

She found Bonderev chain-smoking in Operations. One of the consoles was open, its contents spilling out, a German contractor up to his elbows in fibre optics. He and Bonderev traded insults in French, their only common language. On the ten-metre main wall screen, red lines crawled over a relief map of the Gobi Desert. An inset repeater screen showed a close up NAVSAT image of the area.

Bambera leaned on the balcony rail and watched as Bonderev stubbed out his evil-smelling black cigarette. Around him personnel stepped over cables, junction boxes and crates that littered the floor. With its unnatural light and regulated air, the workers called this room the 'armpit'.

'Bonderev,' called Bambera.

The Russian looked up and gave her a sour look.

'Shall I come down?'

Bonderev shook his head and walked up the stairway. There was a loud Teutonic curse behind him as the Gobi Desert vanished from view in a blaze of visual static.

A squat man in his fifties, Bonderev was out of breath by the time he joined Bambera on the balcony.

'Teething troubles with NAVSAT,' he said, nodding below.

'Who's in the Gobi?' asked Bambera.

'The Ethiopians.' He lit up another cigarette.

'I thought we weren't supposed to use national designations,' said Bambera. 'I read a memo or something.'

Bonderev shrugged. 'It's a tight ground sweep. Meteorite impact.'

'Oh, a rock hunt. Big, was it?'

'Came in out of the eliptic,' he said. 'NAVSAT 81 spotted it. Gargarin Station tracked it down. You know the cosmonauts, very excitable people.' He crossed to his console, ready for her inevitable briefing.

'Who have we got in England?' she said.

He scrolled the answer up. 'Third Light Recce just back from Libya, laid up at Aylesbury.'

'Tell them to have a couple of squads on standby, light weapons. I've got a Dull Sword in south-west England.'

Cyrillic letters rolled up on Bonderev's screen. The big bulk translators in the house above would translate from Russian to English before sending orders to Aylesbury.

Aylesbury, thought Bambera, why is that familiar?

The answer eluded her, but she doubted it was important.

She sat at Bonderev's console and could only come up with one other question. 'The English weather. Is it still hot?'

There was a cheer from below as Operations got the Gobi Desert back.

Surveillance Statellite NAVSAT 61 in geo-stationary orbit at a height of 59.82 miles above North-west Europe, accessed its memory and scanned for a comparative event.

It had identified a Grade 6 burst of neutrino activity in section A9 lasting 0.26 seconds. With no apparent trace source for the emission, NAVSAT 61 sent a routine Talk-to-Me option to NAVSAT 71 stationed over the North Atlantic.

NAVSAT 71 had no record of the emission. It ran a memory check. Suggestion: Comparable event. Possible relation to localized sunspot activity.

NAVSAT 61 withdrew the option of an Italic Alert on the information. Instead it sent a Retainer order to signpost the event for the UNIT Space Surveillance computers at Herstmonceux Control.

The computers recorded the messsage and inserted the relevant Retainer. The unidentified event was sift-selected and the data passed to Geneva HQ, where its print-out was folded neatly into oblivion halfway down a stack of continuous computer paper.

An unbidden alien presence had slipped through the surveillance net, as it had been accustomed to do for longer than the scribes could recall.

The sword Excalibur recognized the neutrino burst at Night Watch plus 1242.192 solar cycles. It also recognized a flare of tachyons and other superlucid particles which NAVSAT 61 could not even begin to notice.

The sword had recorded this activity pattern before. The spells that bound its blade went to pre-alert mode. This phase had been conjured nearly a thousand times, but unless direct contact was made with its secondary alert key, the sword's spell status would return to basic observation mode after 600 seconds.

The new intruder slowly swept a broad scanning probe across the geomass, formulating and assessing the features and contours of the Avallion countryside as it went. It missed the sword's receptors by 159 miles.

300 seconds.

The probe swept back and missed again, recording only the shoreline of the lake.

The sword waited. 500 seconds.

On the third sweep, the probe met Excalibur's open key head on.

Contact. The incantation was complete. The sword's recloaking spell was a closed option. The fire in the pommel amethyst flared.

Magic and logic in conjunction.

Excalibur remembered the like mind of the TARDIS and blasted out a greeting worthy of the 1242.192 years it had waited.

The battered blue police box hovered three miles above the Bristol Channel, a tiny silhouette against the first light of the dawn sky. The Gallifreyan Time and Space ship, an outmoded but still vigorous TARDIS, swayed in its position, compensating for the 15-knot air current at this altitude.

Its systems retrieved major topographical features from previous information and overlaid them on the newly scanned data from its probe. Moments later it was producing an updated map of Britain in the late 1990s.

More industrial development and more water. Several major changes to the structure of the coastline. Two low-lying areas had disappeared below sea level and there were a number of new islands.

At the pilot's request, the TARDIS double-checked that it had marked in a suburban development known locally as Perivale.

The ship's task was almost complete when Excalibur's greeting invocation slammed into its sensory systems. The spell bypassed the initial receiver grid and hit direct into the TARDIS's artron centre like a barrage.

All over the northern hemisphere, radio listeners and TV viewers dashed to turn off their receivers. CB breakers and radio hams tore off their headphones in agony. Telephone users flung down their handsets. Computer systems crashed. The complete NAVSAT surveillance net went dead.

The TARDIS dropped three hundred metres in five seconds and kept dropping. In shock, the ship had channelled all its power into cutting back the barrage. Automatic systems began to shut down.

Amid loud protests from the crew, the lights went out, the ventilation faltered and the sensors died.

The falling TARDIS struggled to regain its senses and failed. Its reflexes were traumatized and its instincts swamped. It was deaf, dumb, blind and its artron mainframe was devoid of a single coherent thought impulse.

The ship pitched gracefully sideways as the barrage greeting drowned out the crew's yells and even the sound of the air that screamed past outside.

The earth was rising eagerly to meet the dead TARDIS when

a sudden surge of energy pulsed through the ship's systems. The assault on its senses began to be countered and contained.

Its first sluggish new thought was a remembrance that it had a pilot who was capable of taking over manual control. At least when he could get the sequences correct.

Override signals and stabilizer inputs flickered urgently into the TARDIS's neural systems. The police box's free fall gradually slowed in response to the pilot's guidance and finally steadied back into hover mode at just two hundred metres above the surface.

With the pilot in control, the ship's artron centre began to think clearly again. But the invocation still pulsed. As other systems were restored, the ship was free to analyze its personal greeting.

'I am here,' said the message in Gallifreyan.

'Identity?' sent the TARDIS.

'Myselfe,' came the response in Early English.

There followed a sequence of runes which the TARDIS language bank did not recognize, but the source clearly assumed that they would be familiar.

The message was transmitting on a wide spread of spectral and extra-spectral frequencies to the exclusion of everything else.

None of the data connected or made sense. But that was routine. The TARDIS was not defeated in its task. It had one further resource to employ. It resumed standard procedure and relayed the message up to its control interface. From there the pilot might deal with it.

Alone in his darkened control room, the Doctor watched an auxiliary screen stop rolling and juddering. While its readout settled slowly back to a safe level, he flicked up three more filter switches in the hope that they might stabilize the energy distribution.

By instinct or symbiosis with his timeship, the Doctor sensed the crisis easing. The TARDIS's convulsion had given him a nasty turn, but although its power still fluxed, he felt the stresses relax like claws letting go of his nerve endings. He cored in two more stabilizers just to be certain.

The crisis had lasted less than two minutes, but the Doctor felt suddenly exhausted. A great weight pressed on his mind, like the whole of the unimaginable future toppling backwards, and he was the only support it had.

He thought to push forward, but feared that the reversed potential might start a Donimo Surge. He saw an uncontrolled ripple of collapsing time, growing infinitely, smashing against every alternative at every second of every future, until the tidal wave plunged the whole of Creation into an empty abyss of Chaos.

He dared not move for fear of what he might start. He was trapped by a hypothetical possibility. But that was the tightrope he walked, balancing precariously across time and space, between one alternative and another, over a pit of a billion more.

He gripped the edge of the control console and took a deep breath. His eardrums still fizzed with the aftereffects of the barrage. He wanted his hat. He would feel better with his panama hat and his paisley scarf.

His grip on the control console tightened. What was he thinking of? Somewhere at the back of his mind, he had the feeling that someone was trying to tell him something, but he could not decide exactly who.

Across the chaos of the dimly lit console room, he saw movement from a tangled heap of furniture by the outer doors. As the ship systems slowly filtered back, it occurred to him that he had a companion.

'Mmph,' said the heap.

A brass church lectern shaped like an eagle lay across the top of the pile. The Doctor tapped it cautiously with his knuckles. There was no response, so he began to prise the heap apart piece by piece — a technique he employed endlessly on the universe at large.

Ace was trapped at the bottom of the pile, pinned under the overturned chair she had been sitting in when the first lurch of the assault hit home. 'I can't hear you,' she complained loudly before the Doctor had even said a word.

'It's only temporary . . . like most things,' he muttered as he helped her up. But it also struck him that the familiar hum of his ship's power systems was unusually quiet — or deliberately restrained. Everything sounded at least two rooms away.

'What? I can't hear you, Professor. I think I've gone deaf.'

She shook out her tangled hair and stuck her fingers in her ears. The blast of sound that had hit her reminded her of the wickedest rock concert she had ever been to. On that occasion she had been deaf for two days — this felt five times worse.

She wondered if Time Lords were required to take a driving test before being let loose on the byways of the universe with an unsupervised time machine. The Doctor always seemed preoccupied with the irrelevant minutiae of his ship, rather than the general business of getting them from A to B in one piece.

He was about to key in a set of tabs, when a loud repetitive pulsing signal emerged from one of the speakers. Instantly, the normal sounds of the TARDIS came back into aural focus.

Ace shook her head again. 'Now what?' she moaned. 'What's going on?'

The Doctor shot the control console an accusing glance. A diagram flickered up on to a monitor. Vector lines diverged like a web in all directions from a central core. Angular runes marked each line, shifting both colour and shape across the wide range of transmission frequencies from the fluting signal.

Ace peered over the Doctor's shoulder at the screen. 'What is that noise?'

'A cry in the dark.'

Already well versed in the Doctor's infuriating habit of keeping everything to himself, she began to draw her own conclusions. 'Distress call?'

'Hmm.'

'Intergalactic Mayday?'

'Possibly. Perhaps a summons. Or a warning. Of course it might be a greeting.'

'It gives me the creeps, whatever it is.'

Just as she began to get some hang of the screen, the Doctor tapped instructions into a keyboard and the whole layout shifted in its perspective.

'Extraordinary,' he said.

The web lengthened out into a wire-frame tunnel down which they travelled. From every section of the frame, new webs of transmission vectors branched out.

'It's covering everywhere at once,' he said. 'And I do mean every conceivable where. Surging out through the cosmos. Forwards in time, backwards in time... and sideways.'

'Sideways!'

'Yes. Across the boundaries that divide one universe from another.'

Ace tried to appreciate that this flowery simplification was for her benefit. She preferred to translate it into something more clearly and scientifically defined.

'So what you're saying is that instead of the usual rectilinear propagation within the normative space/time continuum, this signal's wavefront is omnidirectional along every axis of the temporal continuum.'

'Yes.'

'I still think it's creepy. Who's it for?'

'I don't know!'

'Well, where's it coming from?'

He had already begun to key in a triangulation order, but before he had finished, a small coordinate readout appeared at the foot of the screen. The Doctor raised an eyebrow. 'That's odd. It seems to be coming from Earth.'

'Really? Whereabouts?'

'Not just where... when? What point in time?' He waited as more data began to print out across the screen and then announced, 'Late twentieth-century Earth.'

'It's not coming from Perivale, is it?'

'No,' he said rather too quickly.

'Phew!'

He was slightly surprised as the map he had just been compiling overlaid on the monitor. 'West of London. Now who could be operating a transmitter of such stupendous power in Cornwall?' He began to tap the rhythm of the signal out with his finger against the console.

'Why don't you decode the message?' said Ace.

'I'm positive that the technology isn't right for this time...

19

What was that?'

'Why don't you decode the message or something? Then you'll know who it's from.'

He looked at her, startled by the simplicity of her solution. 'That's brilliant, Ace!' He wondered why he had never thought of it.

Ace made a mental note to state the obvious more often.

The Doctor began to adjust the settings on the console. 'We'll just change the modulation, like so,' he said, suddenly grateful that the TARDIS was filtering out so much of the superfluous transmission.

The signal began to transmute, compressing and then enhancing, echoing around the darkened console room as it fed through the TARDIS computer systems.

'Just twist the envelope a little and play.' He gave the console a final theatrical flourish and the sound vanished altogether.

On the monitor, the wire-frame image went berserk, swerving and spiralling as the tunnel sped faster and faster. The harsh light from the screen grew fiercer, catching the Doctor in its glare and throwing his giant shadow up the wall. Finally the rushing image broke up completely. The message's harsh trill vanished and the screen went dead.

'Merlin!' hissed a sibilant spider-voice from the speakers.

Instinctively, Ace looked across at the Doctor and found him returning her confused stare.

Thunder rumbled in the clear air outside.

Dark thought from another time and place pierced the skies and looked into Avallion's morning. Its eyes sought those who heard the message of the sword.

'At last, he is revealed to us!'

High in the suddenly storm-rich air, the TARDIS sensed the danger. Its systems shuddered.

The first drops of rain began to fall.

Chapter 2

The weathermen were embarrassed.

The violent storm that was wreaking havoc over the south of England had come from nowhere. Worse than the great storms of 1987 and 1995, this time there was not even an inadequate explanation.

At 06.33 hours, exactly the time that the diabolic eruption of deafening sound and static had woken most of Northern Europe, the barometer had dropped like a stone.

Several groups of morbidly eager evangelists took the blasts to be the Last Trump and revelled as all meteorological hell broke loose immediately afterwards.

As the British Met Office computers went down and the lights failed, one hapless systems operator swore that while he fiddled to light a candle, he saw his precious pine cone (which he kept as a reliable fail-safe) opening and closing its segments like an overenthusiastic sea anemone.

The rush hour was at a standstill before it could even start. Warnings spread across the media — for the precious few who could still hear them.

'Stay at home. Don't even attempt to travel. There will be structural damage and flooding.'

The force-twelve hurricane clawed and howled across the countryside like an unleashed demon. Most of the God-fearing British battened down their hatches and sat tight until the storm inevitably tore off their roofs or flooded their front rooms.

The stationary UNIT command car shook under the relentless onslaught of the storm.

Bambera, dressed in DPM combat fatigues, stared at the pounding rain on the windscreen until her eyes ached. It should have been daylight, but it was black as hell outside and visibility was down to zero. The torrential downpour was hitting the roof like a massed corps of drums.

After the Zambezi, England was like the Arctic. It felt like half the night since they had been forced to pull up. They were stuck on an open Cornish road, only three klicks from the nearest village, but at the mercy of these elements, it might as well have been three hundred.

She looked at her watch. 09.21 hours. They had been there two hours and forty-eight minutes and Sergeant Zbrigniev, her driver, was no conversationalist. He had been with UNIT since the old days and had seen a few skirmishes. She knew that from his file. But experience hadn't made him a philosopher. He never talked about how they coped on Bug-Hunts, using firearms that looked like pea-shooters against today's smart strategic weaponry.

Bambera picked up the radio handset again and repeated wearily, 'Salamander Six Zero, this is Seabird One. Are you receiving me?'

A tirade of white noise swamped all frequencies. The entire sane world had shrunken to the confines of the buffeted car. A last tiny illuminated beacon in the raging maelstrom.

Eighteen years OTT, on the tarmac, and she still hated inactivity. Always on alert. Always waiting for orders to go in. She still remembered the Gulf.

Zbrigniev shifted restlessly in the driver's seat. 'We could try moving again, sir. Slowly . . .' His grasp of English was impeccable as ever, but his Polish accent always got thicker under stress.

'Forget it, Zbrigniev, the convoy can't be far ahead. This won't keep up much longer.'

Bambera replaced the handset. There was a heavy crash

outside, followed by a dragging, rustling sound as something like a small tree travelled past the car.

The Dull Sword operation was turning into the sort of nightmare that happened to other COs. Not to her.

She had been trained for and survived worse situations than this. It was the storm that had screwed them up. The planning reports had said nothing about the weather, yet this was the great-grandfather of all storms. An inferno of cold and wet. She had never experienced anything like it.

Nor was there an explanation for the blast of ungodly noise that had immediately preceeded the storm and nearly landed them in a ditch.

Outside, the rain continued to lash down as if this was its last chance before the Sahara.

She put the idea that the storm was unnatural out of her head. That was one of UNIT's occupational hazards: always imagining the weirdest. This wasn't *The Tempest*, this was the night Brigadier Bambera lost a nuclear missile convoy on a peacetime manoeuvre. Shame!

The thunder had become a continuous rumble often lost under the barrage of the gale. Lightning flickered inside the clouds rather than below them, as if an immense war engine was passing slowly overhead.

'Not yet, Zbrigniev. Any chance of coffee?'

'Sorry, sir. We finished the flask.'

She closed her eyes and wished that now and then her adjutant could be a little less formal.

Zbrigniev leaned across and fumbled in the base of the map box. 'Emergency supplies, sir,' he said and produced a large bar of chocolate.

There was a burst of static as the radio crackled back into life. '. . me in Seabird One. Thi. . . . . .alamander Six Zer. . . Are y. . . . . .eiving. Over.'

Lightning fast, Bambera had the handset off its hook.

'Come in Salamander Six Zero. This is Seabird One. Please clarify your position. Over.'

Through the distorted signal she could just about make out the voice of Lieutenant Richards, who was leading the missile convoy. 'Ma..ive elec..cal disturb... Over.'

'You're breaking up, Richards. I repeat, clarify your position. Over.'

'Must ...ave ...ken a wrong turning ...mewhere. NAVSAT is nonoperational. Ov...'

The rain and wind seemed to relent a little. Bambera and Zbrigniev glanced at each other.

'Well, get outside, Richards, and look for a road sign. Use your initiative. Over.'

'Will do, s...'

A massive squawk of interference blanked out the transmission completely. Bambera set down the handset again.

'All right Sergeant, let's move.'

The lightning still arced across the great rift between the universes. It flickered above the low cloudbase that lashed rain in sheets upon Avallion. The thunder was only an echo from another existence.

For a moment the racing wolfclouds tore apart and an eye of infinite blue sky stared through.

'*Soon dominion over all things shall be mine...*'

The storm surged around the TARDIS as it hovered between realities. Its sensors sought out the instigator of the signal. Alternatives. Possibilities. The way was no longer clear.

Which way? Which universe?

The surging blanket of cloud tore against the massive edifice of the High Tagel. White-walled buttresses rose like snow sculptures in the moonlight. Ancient and enduring, vaulted and carved with the shapes of a thousand wings. Ancient halls and galleries of power and council, the bastion of the High King, crowned by a soaring forest of towers and turrets, some bridged by walkways and terraces, all topped with spires of silvered ice.

At its heart stood the symbol of its birth. Carved from a fallen bough of Yggdras, the world tree, ringed by a single bench with room enough to seat one hundred and fifty knights. Arthur's table, at which all men were honoured and equal. Where even the king had no throne.

Still standing after an age, a deep crack ran from the table's heart to its edge, where in later days, the single bench had been cut away to allow for the inclusion of a throne carved from a single block of obsidian. Rank after rank of S'rax battle standards hung from the vaulted ceiling, a tapestry of conquest in azure and scarlet. On the marble wall behind the throne, a map of the heavens was picked out in sapphires and platinum wire.

In this chamber, the council of state assembled at places once reserved fror Arthur's knights. Men and women who had grown old in the service of Deathless Morgaine, as had their forebears, generation after generation for twelve centuries. An alliance of thirteen worlds without end.

A sudden gust of wind stirred the banners. From a region unknown echoed a distant growl that was not thunder.

To the castle's leeward side, through the rent torn like a black banner in the clouds, lay the dark world, beset by storm, lit only by the play of the lightning below.

Lights burned at every window of the High Tagel like the torches of the holy vigil. The castle was awake. It awaited news from the one chamber where no light dared flicker.

Darkness burned in the lowest turret under the Tagel and above the world. Every shadow was summoned and clustered there. Forced and refined by ancient sorcery into a pool of pitch so black that it reflected other worlds for its mistress.

'How long? How long have you kept me in waiting? But I have never relented in my watch. And at last we shall have one final meeting!'

A gateway that overlooked the curving world slid open.

Out of the under vaults of the Tagel swooped a flying machine. It cut an uncertain path, squealing at the inky storm into which it had launched. Finally its Flightsman kerbed the ornithopter's terror and forced its unruly wings to spread with a steady beat.

On a mission of the utmost urgency, the machine sped away across the night.

The Doctor sifted through the heap of books that lay tumbled on the floor of the TARDIS's library. The longevity of the pile was uncertain. The TARDIS had lurched so often lately that it had hardly seemed worth the effort to replace the books on the shelves, especially when another trip to the floor might be imminent at any time.

With a cry of triumph, he extracted a copy of Malory's *Le Morte D'Arthur* from the heap. He blew off the dust. It was Volume I: Books I to IX. Exactly what he wanted. He pocketed the book and headed back to the console room.

As Ace worked amid the debris of the TARDIS laboratory, she heard the note of the ship's engines alter. The Doctor must have finally decided where to take them. Now that they were in real flight again, she didn't have long if the Doctor wasn't to catch her. But he did need someone to watch his back.

She prayed that the TARDIS wouldn't give another of its habitual lurches. This was the delicate bit. Using only her fingertips, she began to ease the tops on to the canisters that contained her latest and most wickedly-volatile-so-far batch of nitro-nine.

Lightning flickered through the windows of the Galing Pard, the furthermost inn of Gore. But the thunder never came. The storm was elsewhere.

'Landlord!' yelled Sir Dornard de Breunis. 'Where's the Prince's ale?'

Mordred stared sullenly into his empty tankard. 'You have no need to shout,' he said. 'You remind me of my mother.'

He always wore a plain jesseraunte on these trips, because even the most daffish peasant would recognize the Prince's armour. But what did that matter now Dornard had given his rank away?

He had spent most of the night drinking and he was still not drunk. But it was better to be in an empty inn on the windswept Westermost marches, than to endure the daily duty of Morgaine's courtly receptions at the High Tagel. Let her put the fear of God into the nobles who paid her fealty if that was what she desired. In the meantime, since she was always too much engaged to talk to him, he would beat the fear of God out of the peasants instead.

'The ale in this inn wouldn't get a fish drunk,' sneered Dornard as the landlord hurried up with another jug. 'Dishwater!' He snatched the vessel out of their host's grasp and hurled it across the room. It smashed to pieces against the firemantel.

Dornard roared with laughter as the landlord trembled before them. 'Bring us something better!'

Mordred just snorted. He was growing weary of Sir Dornard de Breunis. They had drunken and wenched together since Dornard had first become a bachelor knight, but the Prince's latest crony was getting old. Dornard was growing a girth like a larded pig with too little adventure and too much ale. His mind had turned sluggish amongst the stews around the Tagel barracks. He no longer made Mordred laugh. His wild behaviour, once a foil to Mordred's own, was now vulgar and gross in one of advancing age.

Dornard was nearing thirty.

It was time for Mordred to find new drinking companions.

This was no new thing for the Prince. Nothing was new. The thirteen worlds prospered and changed little under the rule of Deathless Morgaine.

Nor did they change for her son.

Mordred, Crown Prince-in-waiting to an immortal mother. But he was immortal too, with appetites that were always young. The Battle Queen's gift to her son.

Always in waiting. Always bored. Thirteen worlds without end.

He needed young heads around him with the new amusements they might bring. But drinking companions came and grew old as quick as summer flies. Nothing ever changed.

'Yes, fetch me something better, landlord.' The Prince held up a single gold bezant.

The host's eyes widened. 'What can I bring, my lord?'

'I hear you have a daughter...'

'Lord Prince...' he stuttered. 'She's my only child!'

'Have a care, landlord, or I'll have you fetch her mother for my fat friend here!'

'But my lord...' The little man tried to meet the prince's dark eyes, but his will was broken. He scuttled for his kitchen.

'And more ale. Proper ale!' yelled Mordred. He was cold tonight. Something like the choleric bile dulled his soul. For no apparent reason, an old memory of Merlin repeatedly mocked at his thoughts.

Dornard waited for his Prince to laugh, but there was not so much as a sneer. The drunken knight leant forward and laid his head on the table amid the empty mugs.

A low trill sounded from Mordred's discarded helmet. The Grade 2 summon/warning alarum that he had ignored all night had moved up to Grade 1.

He struggled to his feet, sword in hand. He was drunker than he had thought. Beside him, Dornard lay face down, grumbling in his stupor.

The inn door swung open and a figure in the livery of a Royal Flightsman pushed inside. When she saw the swaying prince, she came smartly to attention and saluted.

'Your highness, I have sealed orders from the queen.'

The relay capsule she took from her jerkin was imprinted with Morgaine's seal. Mordred pulled on his armoured helmet and fumbled to fit the relay into the receptor plate.

The incantation was simple. It needed only his name spoken in his voice to break the seal.

The Flightsman waited as she heard the Prince begin to laugh. Then he lifted his visor. He was half sober again already.

'Your ornithopter. Is it flight-ready?'

'Yes, your highness.'

'Then let's be away from this ratsty.' He tossed the gold bezant down on the table and left Sir Dornard asleep among the last dregs of their friendship.

28

Chapter 3

Spring had been postponed.

The roads were slippery with the wet green leaves stripped from the trees by the storm. Zbrigniev's training took each obstacle of debris in its stride, but although the onslaught had died, the UNIT car never topped fifteen miles an hour.

Since radio contact with the convoy had given out again, Bambera gleaned what information she could on a static-ridden line to UNIT's London Centcomp. The country was in chaos. Most of the midlands were without electricity and many roads were impassable. They were lucky to be moving at all.

She lost contact just as the command car came to an abrupt halt where a fallen oak had blocked the road.

Zbrigniev backed up until he found a side turning into a narrow wooded lane. The corner verge was churned to mud, a sure sign that they had found the convoy's new route.

Bambera tried the radio again; it was still dead. But she reckoned that she might have a chance of finding the convoy before she'd had to report its loss.

Zbrigniev was already growing accustomed to the stillness that followed the storm. Nature seemed stunned by the ferocity of its own outburst. A sudden movement along the road ahead was doubly surprising.

'Brigadier.'

'What now?' she complained.

'Hitchhikers.'

Bambera had a brief glimpse of two figures as they passed. A long-haired girl in black with her thumb out and a glare of contempt on her face, and an older man in a straw hat.

'Shame,' she said and the car sped on.

The Doctor noted the new winged globe insignia as the UNIT car passed, before he returned his attention to the small tracking device he was carrying.

'Don't stop then, I don't care!' yelled Ace after the vehicle. She turned back in disgust to the Doctor. 'What year are we in?'

'Near the end of the twentieth century.'

'Can't you be more specific? Eighties or nineties?'

The Doctor stared up at the cloudless sky and frowned. 'On the grand scale of things, Ace, what's a decade?' He set off along the lane, unconcerned by the mud and puddles.

A Range Rover turned the corner behind them.

'Professor!'

The Doctor kept walking. 'I don't suppose it'll stop, Ace.'

'Don't be such a pessimist, Professor. Ace stuck out her thumb anyway and the car pulled over beside her. The tax disc in the window said 30.6.99.

Doubling back with a satisfied smile, the Doctor said, 'Of course being a pessimist has its extra share of pleasant surprises.'

Carbury Trust was stencilled on the car door. The driver's window wound down and the genial face of a grey-bearded man in his late fifties studied them.

'Good morning. Need a lift?' he said in a northern accent.

'Thank you very much,' said the Doctor, eyeing the dark shape sitting on the back seat.

'Hop in the back.' The driver unlocked the door and added, 'Don't mind Cerberus. Just push him out of the way.'

The Doctor was already climbing inside. He was about to raise his hat to the other occupant, when he found himself nose to nose with a large Irish wolfhound.

Ace took one look and decided to sit in the front with the driver.

'Move over Cerberus, you great hulk,' he said and pushed

30

the wolfhound out of the way.

'Nice doggie,' added the Doctor. He looked enviously into the front where Ace was already belting up. Cerberus looked at the Doctor and panted loudly in his ear.

'I take it you were caught in the storm,' said the driver as he pulled the Range Rover away.

'Storm?' asked Ace.

'Yes, you're right. Storm is an understatement. But then the weathermen never allow us the luxury of a hurricane, do they? I don't think I've ever seen anything quite like this one though. Bizarre.' He swerved to avoid a fallen branch.

'Oh yes, the storm,' agreed the Doctor, adjusting his tracking device. 'Nasty noisy thing.'

'Ferocious, more like. Plenty of damage around too. You must have found somewhere decent to shelter. Where were you heading?'

The Doctor looked at his tracker. 'North-east.'

'Heading for the dig, eh?'

'An archaeological dig?'

'Yes, I'm on my way now to check that it's still there!' He glanced amiably at the Doctor via the driving mirror. 'I'm sorry, I haven't introduced myself. Doctor Peter Warmsly. I'm site manager for the Carbury Trust Conservation Area.'

The Doctor opened his mouth to answer and Ace said, 'I'm Ace and this is the Doctor.'

'Another doctor, eh? What of? Science? Medicine? Philosophy?'

'Just a Doctor,' said the Doctor.

'Ah . . .' The car slowed to negotiate the gap left by a fallen beech which covered most of the road. The topmost twigs scraped along the car's flank. 'Of course the dig is just a hobby.'

'Of course,' said the Doctor.

'It was a battlefield judging from the patterns of arrowheads and the disposition of the bones. From about the eighth century . . .'

Cerberus, who was slobbering on to an elegant handkerchief that the Doctor had placed apprehensively over his trews, pricked up his ears, scrambled to his not inconsiderable full

31

height on the back seat and barked. The other passengers were practically deafened.

'Be quiet, you wretched hound!' Peter took a blind swipe behind at his dog and narrowly missed the Doctor.

Cerberus clambered over the Doctor and planted his nose against the open gap at the top of the window. He gave a muted whine which mingled with the distant scream of air as something hurtled to earth nearby.

'I hate that sound,' complained Peter. 'Sometimes I lie awake at night thinking it might be . . .'

'The start of something terrible,' interjected the Doctor as he struggled out from under the dog.

There was the dull roar of an impact explosion. Ace flinched in the front seat. 'What was it?'

'The military use the area as a firing range. I've never understood why.'

The Doctor peered out of the mud-flecked window. He pointed his tracker device in the direction of the explosion. It registered a high burst of chronon particle activity; not the sort of thing normally associated with clodhopping military manoeuvres.

'Blowing the occasional chunk out of the ground keeps them amused,' he said to reassure the others.

Ace twisted round in her seat to look at him. 'It didn't sound like a shell.'

'No.' He gesticulated vaguely with the tracker. The signal was coming from over the next ridge. He wondered who or what else it might have attracted.

The knight's black jesseraunte lifted him slowly out of the smoking impact crater.

The leap had been simple. It was the armoured suit that leapt, not the leaper. And it was the suit that carried him high into the upper atmosphere, leaving the bright world behind; up above the clouds, far beyond the hovering, turretted Tagels into the star-sprinkled sky; along the silver arc between realities.

And as the muscled joints of the suit began to wail in protest, the forces of gravity tore against the vaulting escape velocity.

Then in a glorious moment of planned inspiration, the suit slipped between the two grappling energies, sideways into another existence.

The leaper laughed at its simplicity.

The shade of the world shifted from darker to paler blue. The cloud patterns swirled into new forms. The leaper began to fall headlong, the ablative shield of his armour seething white-hot in the atmosphere. Back to the world; not his world, but his world changed. To Avallion, the Isle of Apples, the ordained battlefield.

The air had screeched around the jesseraunte. The velocity energy of the impact exploded out in a roaring plume of flame.

Runes and figures danced on the inside of the black knight's visor as the silver filigree of his armour surveyed the new world he had just entered.

Rumours had been rife in the corridors of the High Tagel: a summons from the older time. And he must seek out the voice that called across the spaces between worlds. He was the knight errant and this was the quest. He had his own past to serve as well. The burden that his parage bore down the centuries passed from vat-father to vat-father until its fulfilling rested with him. But he must be swift. His quest wore no favours. He would be missed by now. Errant absence without leave. But family bonds were ever knotted tighter than oaths of knightly allegiance.

Others would soon follow to answer the summons. And they would welcome his presence as an excuse to be rid of him for ever.

The Range Rover had pulled out of the storm-battered woods and was driving across a high open heathland area, bright with purple heather. As they topped the ridge, the Doctor and Ace saw the lake spread below them like dark rippled glass.

Peter broke into a smile that was almost possessive. 'There you are. Vortigern's Lake!' he announced proudly.

Aha, thought the Doctor and checked that he still had the copy of Malory in his pocket.

Ahead they could see the military car that had ignored them

33

earlier. It was slowly negotiating its way down a lower road.

'What the blazes?' Peter brought his Range Rover sharply to a halt. He climbed out of the car and stared angrily down the hill towards the lake edge.

The Doctor and Ace heard a string of undefined expletives as they joined him.

The road running down to the edge of Vortigern's Lake rapidly turned into a rough track. A number of military vehicles the colour of muddy khaki were grouped on the edge of the bank: several jeeps, a heavy-duty lorry and a large van which the Doctor recognized as a Command Trailer.

Close by, cut into the green turf running inland from the lake, was an earth-brown rectangle. In its shape, small methodically-worked areas had filled with rainwater to form square puddles.

They could see a group of squaddies working around the lorry under arc lamps, apparently trying to dig its back wheels out of the mud. As the UNIT car approached, an officer broke from the group and went to meet its occupants.

Without a word, Peter Warmsly turned, walked back to his car and climbed inside.

'We'll walk down from here,' called the Doctor, but the Range Rover was already heading away down the hill. 'I think he's worried about his dig,' he said apologetically to Ace.

She ignored him. The squaddies by the lake had briefly lifted the tarpaulin which covered the heavy lorry. The tail fin she had glimpsed underneath gave her a cold chill. 'Professor, it's a missile convoy.'

The Doctor aimed the tracker down the hill and squinted with one eye through a small glass sight. 'It's a nuclear missile convoy.'

'How do you know?'

'It has a graveyard stench.'

At first he aimed the tracker directly at the convoy: the source of the signal was there. But that was ridiculous. Typical soldiers, he thought, always getting in the way. He wondered how far UNIT had come since the days of Alastair Lethbridge-Stewart. Probably coldly technological and characterless without the Brigadier's inimitable personality. Yet they should certainly be above playing with out-dated nuclear missiles.

He stabbed irritably at the scanner keys and tried again: no difference. In a sudden flash, he realized that the source of the signal was located beyond the convoy. The transmissions were coming from the lake itself.

The sense of relief with which Lieutenant Richards, seconded from the Royal Welch Fusiliers, greeted the Brigadier was tainted with foreboding. Bambera had the reputation of a martinet. Twice as hard because she was a black woman with twice as much to prove. He saluted sharply, praying that his mudcaked uniform might work in his favour.

Bambera made a brief inspection of the damage, noting the smashed sign marked *Carbury Trust*. 'That'll be trouble,' she said.

The smell of diesel was strong. Eleven of the sixteen wheels on the missile launch vehicle were buried in the mud at the lake's edge. The two rear axles were smashed.

'Oh, very good. Why not drive it right into the lake?'

Richards glanced at Sergeant Zbrigniev, who had been following in the Brigadier's tracks. He kept a fixed stare on the ground.

'All right, Richards,' said Bambera. 'Extreme circumstances. We nearly landed in a ditch too.'

'Sir,' he said with relief.

'Let's just get this thing out of here before the ratpack gets wind of it.'

She mounted the steps of the command trailer. The interior was comfortably functional. The walls lined with Panyuko-Mishkin communication stations and missile control decks. A Japanese sparks was at work on one of the panels.

Bambera pulled off her beret and sank into a deep leather swivel chair. 'What I need, Richards, is a large shot of coffee.'

'No sugar, no milk, sir.' He nodded to the soldier on brew up duty.

Good man, she thought, he's been taking to Zbrigniev.

From overhead, there was a whooshing scream of air followed by a distant explosion.

'What was that?'

'Low flying jet?' suggested Richards.

'Not unless they're looking for us. Can you check Centcomp for flightpaths yet?'

The sparks looked round and shook his head. 'Sorry sir, still can't get a signal out past a two-klick radius. It's just white noise right across the dial.'

Bambera wondered who'd started a war without telling her.

'Excuse me, sir.' Zbrigniev was standing in the door. 'There's a Doctor Warmsly out here who wants to talk to someone in charge.'

'Already? That was fast.' She turned to her lieutenant. 'You talk to him, Richards, and get him away from here. We have enough trouble as it is.'

The storm had tangled the branches of a fallen tree with a mass of briar making the path impenetrable. The Black Knight drew the sword from his back scabbard and began to cut his way through.

He had heard the inward flight of the first scout which heralded a larger party. The signal he followed was growing weaker and he had no chart to find his way. No man had visited Avallion for generations past. But he had leapt the chasm, and the joy of that sustained him; for there was little joy here.

This place called Avallion was a fitting battlefield. It had grown neglected and cankered. Yet the homelands he had spurned prospered and bloomed full fair for those who served the tyrant queen. Even his own family at Garde-Joyeuse paid Deathless Morgaine tribute through fear. But at what price had she gained such dark power? They said her sorcery had cost her her soul. And how many other souls had she pledged in blood for the world?

The air screamed again and he saw vapour trails in the cold sky. Seconds later, he heard the impact explosions. Time was catching him up. Positions were being staked. The battle lines were being drawn. It would be a final glorious battle between the past and the present. The present had already arrived. But he was summoned by the past, by the oath he had inherited and sworn when he reached manhood. And he was his father and all his forebears in one.

He set his sword to the thicket afresh and hacked at a new path.

Chapter 4

The air coming from the lake was dank. A group of squaddies had strung a tape barrier around the convoy and across the track. Ace and the Doctor watched from a distance as Peter Warmsly remonstrated vigorously with them, pointing repeatedly to the dig area seventy-five metres to the east. The phrase most frequently reiterated was 'bloody vandals!'.

The air screeched twice over and the explosions echoed round the hills that enclosed the lake.

'They're not shells,' insisted Ace. 'There're more like rockets.'

'Meteorites,' said the Doctor.

'Really?'

He had been conducting an extended pocket-slapping session which had dislodged a jumble of gadgets and oddments from his deceptively lightweight jacket. Eventually, in his hat, he found a pair of plastic-coated cards.

'I never thought I'd need these again.' He offered one to Ace. 'This should remove a few obstacles.'

She looked at the ID. It was stamped UNIT with a logo different to the signs painted on the vehicles. The photo showed a woman aged about thirty with shoulder-length honey-coloured hair.

The Doctor had set off along the track.

'Who's Elizabeth Shaw?' called Ace, hurrying to keep up.

'She doesn't look anything like me!'

The card's expiry date was 31.12.75.

'Never mind that. Just act like a physicist.'

'But...'

To her astonishment, they marched purposefully past the guards who were dealing with Dr Warmsly, through the scattered convoy vehicles and had almost reached the command vehicle before anyone even noticed.

The next thing she knew, they were surrounded by a group of large and bolshy-looking soldiers.

The Doctor smiled, raised his hat and proffered the ID cards. 'Take me to your commanding officer,' he said.

'Bring them up here,' called a woman's voice.

Ace saw a woman with African features disappear inside the door of the command vehicle. She had been carrying a foam cup which probably contained hot coffee.

'Excellent,' said the Doctor and marched up the steps without waiting to be shoved. Inside the vehicle, he noted the woman's hard stare and the three stars and a crown on her epaulettes that marked out her rank.

'Now, Brigadier, what seems to be the problem?' he said.

The sparks looked round in astonishment. Ace smirked.

'Excuse me?' snapped the Brigadier.

The Doctor looked round at the banks of hissing instruments. 'Well, a massive systems failure caused by an induced power overload. An EMP perhaps.'

'An Electromagnetic Pulse Effect,' said Ace.

'Caused by?'

'A nuclear detonation... usually.'

The Brigadier gritted her teeth. These two were like a double act. 'I think I would have noticed a nuclear explosion.'

'They are conspicuous,' agreed the Doctor and handed over the two ID cards.

Ace frowned. 'If there was no nuke where did the energy pulse come from?'

'Exactly,' he said and produced his tracking device again. But he could not see the lake from here.

The Brigadier looked at the cards with disbelief and then

passed them to her sergeant. The intruders were causing her a lot of aggravation. She reckoned it was a press stunt and curbed in her temper with difficulty.

'All systems were the result of a minor technical difficulty. Now I don't know where you got these cards from, but I intend to find out!' She nodded to the soldier by the door. 'Escort these two outside and hold them there.'

Finding a firm hand on his shoulder, the Doctor insisted, 'Before I go I'd just like to say three things.'

'What!'

He was being hustled through the door. 'Yeti, Autons, Daleks...' He was already outside. 'Cybermen and Silurians!' he shouted in vain.

Ace nearly tumbled down the steps after him. 'That was five,' she said.

The Doctor scowled. 'Amongst all the varied wonders of the universe, nothing is more firmly clamped shut than the military mind!'

He looked out at the grey lake, where he reckoned the trouble was really coming from. When he glanced back at Command Vehicle, the sergeant was standing in the door. He was holding the ID cards and looking down at the Doctor with marked curiosity.

'Zbrigniev,' called the Brigadier's voice. The sergeant vanished. The Doctor smiled half-heartedly at their guard, dug into his pockets and found an individual packet of broken ginger biscuits. He tore open the top and offered the assortment of fragments to Ace.

'Well done, Zbrigniev. Two civilians waltz up with a pair of antiquated passes and get let in. Why?'

'Sir?' The sergeant looked more confused than sheepish, which is not what she would have expected. Something was going on. Bambera leaned forward in her chair.

'You know something. What is it?'

He looked more awkward than ever and fiddled nervously with the ID cards. 'Off the record, sir.'

'Off the record.'

'Well, sir... When I served under Brigadier Lethbridge-Stewart, we had a scientific adviser called the Doctor.'

'The man outside?'

'No sir, but...' He looked down at the card again and shook his head.

'But?'

Zbrigniev took the plunge. 'He changed his appearance, sir. Twice.'

'A disguise?'

'No, sir. The word was that he changed his whole physical appearance and his personality too... sir.' He saw her look of annoyance and quickly held out the ID cards again.

'Elizabeth Shaw. She worked with the Doctor for a while.'

'Yes,' said Bambera.

'And this was the Doctor. This is the first one with the white hair. Only then he changed, really changed to a man with curly brown hair. Much more eccentric too, sir. But they always said it was the same man. The same Doctor.'

Bambera had been trained to take this in her stride. She closed her eyes.

'Go at everything with an open mind.' Chunky Gilmore had said that repeatedly in lectures. 'Even if it's impossible, treat it with an open mind. If you don't, then you'll be in the sanatorium so fast they'll hear the sonic boom in Coal Hill.'

Lectures at Sandhurst. Now it came back to her. Aylesbury. UNIT's Zen Brigade based at Aylesbury. Brigadier Lethbridge-Stewart.

'How could he be the same man if his appearance changed?'

Now Zbrigniev did look sheepish. 'Don't know, sir.'

'And did Lethbridge-Stewart trust this "Doctor"?'

'With his life, sir.'

The night after they bought the apple tree, Doris dreamt of thunder. She had woken to the sound of wind-driven rain against the window. Lightning flickered in a line under the curtains. The bed was half empty, but still warm from his body. He always rose early, it was an old habit. She lay quietly, listening to the rain and for some hint of his presence in the house.

41

Thunder rolled in the distance.

Doris had inherited the house from her aunt, a mock Tudor extravagance set in half an acre off the A23 near Pyecombe. It was far too large a house for a single woman on her own, but Doris had kept it all the same. Perhaps fate had ordained it — as Alastair pointed out, a peculiar attitude for an economist.

The television had been on, she remembered, more for company in the empty house than for entertainment. She had been reviewing the proof copy of *The Management Crisis in British Industry*, when she looked up and saw his face on the screen.

'*This man knows,*' said the narrator.

Doris dropped her highlighter pen. A telephoto shot of a tall thickset man with a moustache and an erect military carriage, walking the gravel path in front of a Regency mansion.

'*Brigadier Lethbridge-Stewart once held a senior command in a secret military force which operates free of the control of the British government.*'

She was watching the infamous *State Secret* documentary; the one delayed while the Special Branch raided television offices in Birmingham and questions were asked in the House of Commons.

Doris's pen spread a circle of orange on her skirt as she watched.

'*This man knows.*'

In the morning, Doris was on the M1, pressing the accelerator on her old diesel saloon until the car shook.

She found him making tea in the converted prefab that served as his home in the school grounds. Her soldier reduced to a maths master. She was terrified he wouldn't recognize her.

'Good lord,' he said as he opened the door. 'Doris, how marvellous to see you. And I thought it was another of those blasted journalists.'

'*We may never know what happened at the atomic installation at Wenley Moor, the fate of Mars Probe 7, the Styles Conference on disarmament or the terrible ecological accident at Llanfair-fach. But we do know that Brigadier Alastair Lethbridge-Stewart was a leading agent in the Government's response to these crises.*'

None of his precision had left him, even when it came to making the tea. The pot warmed. Two cups placed exactly on a tin tray. An open packet of biscuits set neatly in the middle of the plate. Just as she remembered it from long ago in a Brighton hotel overlooking the seafront. The rain fell against the window and the cold grey sea crashed on the shingle.

They were older, but nothing had really changed. 'Marry me,' she said as he placed the tray before her.

'Of course,' said Alastair and sat down opposite. 'When term finishes.'

The clink of cups broke her reverie as he returned to the bedroom. Reassured, she snuggled back down under the duvet.

'Did you hear that infernal racket?' he said as he placed the tray on the bedside table. 'Can't get a thing on the radio.'

'What racket?' she muttered.

'Like all hell breaking loose.'

She snuggled deeper into the warm bed. 'I must have slept through it.'

'Extraordinary.' He climbed back into bed and dozed contentedly while the tea brewed.

The blue box beside the track hummed perceptibly as the Black Knight ran his hand along its carved contours. Sensors in the mail glove passed the data into the armour's memory book. Illuminated runescript read out across the inside of the umberere visor. The artefact was unknown.

He pushed up his prattling visor. The thrill that had brought the knight up in his tracks was undiminished. Here in the tangled woodland, a world away from the world, was an object he knew from tapestries and old tales. There was little doubt. The past had summoned him and here was its token. And if this was truly Merlin's long-lost ship returned, what other wonders also waited in these wild woods? Wonders which Morgaine's men would stop at naught to destroy.

He heard an angry growl approaching and took refuge among the trees to watch. An armoured cart or chariot carrying three passengers sped past along the track.

So the peasants of Avallion had machines as well. But

compared with those in the world, this graceless and brutish carriage seemed more dead than alive. An ill or good omen? They said that only in a time of greatest need would the High King return to set the worlds to right. The knight turned back to the blue box. That time must be soon if the king's greatest councillor came as his forerunner.

'Why are you driving us to the village?' asked the Doctor from the UNIT vehicle's front passenger seat. From the back, Ace watched the TARDIS disappear into the distance.

Bambera showed no sign of being anything other than very wary of her charges. It was clear that this Doctor knew too much, but he was too upfront to be an enemy agent. Until she could get a clear idea of his identity, and that meant getting radio communication back on line, she was giving nothing away. 'To get you away from Vortigern's Lake.'

'Oh yes, Vortigern. How interesting.'

'Fascinating,' complained Ace. They couldn't be in that much trouble or they'd have had an armed escort.

Bambera's stare hardened on the road. If the convoy was threatened, the last thing she wanted was civilians getting in the way, whoever Zbrigniev thought the Doctor was. In the current scenario, she was the only one who could be spared, and that annoyed her. She took the turning that led down towards Carbury village.

'What's your name?' asked the Doctor.

'What's yours?'

'He's called the Doctor and I'm called Ace,' butted in the voice from the back.

'Brigadier Winifred Bambera,' said the driver.

Ace was astonished. 'Winifred?'

The Doctor nodded. 'There are a lot of secrets held in a name. For example, Vortigern in Old English means High King. So your missile convoy is stranded by the Lake of the High King.'

'It's not my convoy and it's not stranded. It's merely suffering from a minor technical malfunction.'

'If it's so minor, why is UNIT involved?'

'Why are you so interested?'

The Doctor was happy to keep this up for the rest of the trip. 'Why do you care?'

Ace leaned through the gap between them and said, 'Why don't I understand what you two are talking about?'

The Doctor went quiet and looked out at the ravaged countryside. Forces were at play there and he wanted to know who and what their motives were.

Ahead he could see the tiny village of Carbury. Beyond it, the storm's blast had combed the trees flat in one sweep across the hillside.

And Winifred is a modern English equivalent of Guenever.

By the roadside was a half fallen sign marked *The Gore Crow Hotel. Fully Licensed. Non-Residents Welcome.*

Bambera pulled into the drive and stopped in front of the rambling edifice.

'You can stay here,' she said and released the locks on the doors. 'I'll see you later.'

Ace and the Doctor climbed out on to the gravel. 'Thanks for the lift,' called the Doctor raising his hat. 'Good luck with your missile.'

Bambera gave him a glare of contempt and pulled away, narrowly avoiding the brightly-coloured car that was chugging up the drive towards them.

The Chinese girl at the wheel smiled at them as she parked her blue 2CV in front of the hotel. Shou Yuing had to look twice at Ace's clothes to believe them. Surely nostalgia for the eighties wasn't back in fashion again? She'd come home from Exeter University for the Easter vac to get away from fashion victims like that.

'Good morning,' called the Doctor raising his hat again.

Shou Yuing looked at his muddy shoes and grinned back. 'Quite a storm, wasn't it?'

'Yes, it must have been.' He turned and hurried Ace in through the hotel's porch.

The oak-panelled hall smelt of beeswax and freshly cut narcissi. It was deserted, but the sound of an electronic till led them into the bar which seemed to double as a reception area.

There were assorted archaeological fragments around the

walls and a fake fire burning in the real stone fireplace. Beside it, a middle-aged woman sat in an armchair, her hand resting on the open page of a book. She looked up expectantly as the Doctor and Ace walked in. Ace thought she was listening rather than looking.

'Can I help you, sir?' said the friendly-looking man working at the till behind the bar. The woman lowered her head again, reassured.

Pat Rowlinson had not expected customers at all after the storm. Three trees were down in the hotel garden and one chimney pot was lost. He had spent half the morning sizing up damage to the fences and chasing out wallabies from the local woodland colony. Worse than sheep, wallabies. The storm had upset Elizabeth and he hoped that they might have a day off.

'Yes, thank you,' said the Doctor, smiling genially. 'I'd like to book two rooms please. One for myself and another for my young friend.'

'Yes, sir. I don't imagine you've come far today.'

The Doctor looked thoughtful. 'Quite a distance, as it happens.'

Ace leaned in. 'What about a drink, Professor?'

'Why not?' The Doctor scrutinized the rows of bottles behind the bar. 'What have you got?'

Elizabeth Rowlinson smiled as she heard her husband begin his favourite spiel to a new audience.

'What we have sir, is possibly the finest beer in the area, even if I do say so myself. Perhaps the best in the country.'

'Really,' said the Doctor, impressed.

'He makes it himself,' said Shou Yuing as she sat down along the bar by Ace. 'In a converted barn at the end of the garden.'

'It's in the CAMRA guide,' Pat went on. 'We call it Arthur's Ale.'

The Doctor considered for a moment and then said, 'Water please. Straight glass.'

'It's made from the finest local organically-grown ingredients,' insisted Pat.

'Yes. Glass of water please. What do you want Ace?'

She was about to risk the ale, but she caught the Doctor's

eyebrows furrowing sternly, so she said, 'I'll have a lemonade.'

Pat turned away defeated. Ace felt a nudge on the arm.

'Good choice,' giggled Shou Yuing.

'That bad?'

She nodded.

'Have you got any crisps?' called Ace.

'Plain, roasted peanut, onion gravy or cauliflower cheese flavours.'

'Plain.'

Pat turned back with the drinks and crisps. 'Hello, Shou Yuing. What'll it be?'

'Half a cider.'

Ace and Shou Yuing watched as the Doctor began another of his pocket-slapping sessions. He eventually dumped a disparate selection of coins on the counter.

'Four pounds ninety-five please, sir.'

Ace's jaw hit the counter.

'Inflation,' muttered the Doctor. They watched as he sorted out Pallistratum Gromits from seven-and-three-eighth Rlarix Sovereigns. Something shaped like a small mechanoid crab sidled out of the pile of coins and headed across the bar.

The Doctor slapped away Shou Yuing's hand as she tried to poke the object. 'Do you mind, that's a very valuable piece of currency!'

He pocketed the little crustacean and paid Pat for the drinks with a 1998 five pound ecucoin.

Chapter 5

As Bambera turned along the road leading to Vortigern's Lake, her car communicator cracked into life. Things were looking up. She snapped the mike from its cradle and put a direct access to Centcomp.

The line clicked and a woman's voice said, 'Centcomp here. State request and authority. Over.'

'Authorization: Toni-Cade-Sigma. Search subject, male. The Doctor, reference UNIT UK, Yeti, Cyberman, Auton, Dalek, Lethbridge-Stewart. Over.'

'Standby Seabird. Over.'

Nine seconds, enough to irritate Bambera, passed before the clipped voice returned. 'Results: The Doctor. Registration Doctor Smith, John. Designation Scientific Adviser UNIT UK under Brigadier Alastair Gordon Lethbridge-Stewart. Over.'

'Is that it? Over.'

The voice, which might have been a synthvox until then, dropped its formal tone and said apologetically, 'Just about, Seabird. Looks like it's a Hot FR/OG. Except that there's a note that says to look out for a blue police box. Seventies type...'

Bambera stared at the blue police box, seventies type, that she was just passing. The rest of the message was lost as she jammed on her brakes. She signed out from Centcomp and went to investigate.

The air had turned mild, but the woods were deathly quiet. Too quiet. Bambera drew her Browning automatic.

The police box was at an odd angle to the road and its door faced into the trees. Around its perimeter, the young grass was crushed. The box was pitted with scratches and scorch marks. One diamond shape hole resembled an arrow mark.

An impulse made her turn; there was a suit of armour standing a metre from her. Dull black with an emblem of entwined leaves embossed on the breastplate. Not merely a protective suit, but elegant in its lethal functionality: a thing to be worn with pride. Battered, but at one with its wearer. Only the black faceless visor reflected back the rain-sharpened sunlight. The suit's silver filigreed arm pointed a heavy-duty handgun directly at her.

They faced each other for moments across gun sights. Bambera knew she was defenceless against such armour. But did the knight know that? Neither of them moved.

A twig snapped fifty metres away.

Instictively, Bambera flung herself behind the van as its rear left wheel exploded into strings of hot rubber.

There was a deep boom behind her. She saw the Black Knight firing into the woods from the cover of the police box.

As the shells exploded among the trees, he stepped out from his cover and holstered the gun. Bambera watched him draw his sword and advance into the road. Apparently greetings had been exchanged and, as if by some unknown formal ritual, the real fighting could now begin.

A knight clad in plain grey armour burst from the bushes and ran yelling at his enemy. They circled for a second and then hurled themselves together in a clash of steel as their swords met overhead.

Forcing each other apart, they circled again, intent on meeting each other's moves like players in a deadly game. But Bambera could see how every lunge of the Grey Knight was met with an easy parry. The Black Knight's swordplay was instinctive. His opponent fought by schooled method and was clumsy in comparison. He seemed reluctant to attack again, content merely to tease.

Then she saw his method. Another Grey Knight was emerging

49

from the bushes between her and the Black Knight.

As he raised his gun to take the Black Knight from behind, Bambera emptied eight rounds from her automatic into his back.

The bullets pinged uselessly off the armour.

Swinging round, the knight aimed his gun at Bambera instead. With a yell, the Black Knight rammed him sprawling across the road. Then he turned, kicked the feet out from under his first opponent and loped away into the woodland.

Bambera watched as the others scrambled to their feet. Ignoring her completely, they charged after their true quarry. She was astonished by their metal-clad grace.

She walked back to the command car and looked at the melted back wheel. Shame.

Inside, she found her automatic rifle, a 5.65 mm Fa-Mas. The radio was out again, but UNIT HQ would know the scenario by now and would be taking action.

She shouldered the rifle and set off walking towards the village and transport.

The weather had relented its onslaught by 10.30, allowing Doris and the Brigadier to inspect the damage to the garden. The trees were half-naked of leaves and there was a tile missing on a south-facing gable. The daffodils were flattened, but otherwise damage was minimal.

Since it had turned into a warm, bright morning, the Brigadier worked over the ground for the new apple tree. With the changing climate, Doris had considered something more exotic, perhaps a peach. But the Brigadier was a traditionalist and they both liked apple pie.

'In your soldier days, you wouldn't have had to do that yourself,' she said.

He smiled. 'Sergeant Benton. Tree planting party at the double. Step to it, man!'

There were some bedding plants to deal with as well. He made a conscious effort not to put them in a row, because Doris would accuse him of regimenting the garden.

'What's the good of trying for a cottage garden effect if you lay the place out like Trooping the Colour?'

He fiddled with the dial on the portable television. Fierce bursts of static-like interference from a new storm obliterated the Test score. Yet the sky was cloudless and there was no breeze. He had a nagging premonition that England were 36 for 8 against the Russian touring team.

Perhaps he would drive Doris across to Arundel tomorrow for the second day's play — if the match lasted that long.

As it was, there was a pleasant restaurant overlooking Chichester Bay, where the harbour had been before the sea flooded the water meadows. They could always have lunch there.

'Alastair, phone for you.' She was standing by the french windows with the radiophone.

'Who is it?' He barely straightened up.

'It's Geneva.'

He frowned. Now what? Another reunion? Another peace conference? Another interview on the 'Today' programme? Didn't they ever let go? He looked at the little plants in the seed tray. 'Tell them I've retired,' he called. 'Tell them I've decided to fade away.'

He heard her apologizing and saying goodbye. Moments later, she was beside him, her hand on his shoulder.

'Alastair, that was the General-Secretary.'

He stood up effortfully. His past always made her uneasy. That was why she talked about it incessantly. Well, he could soon settle her mind. 'I don't care if it was the king. I'm still retired.' He pointed down at the petunias. 'What do you think?'

'He said something about the Doctor being back.'

Lethbridge-Stewart straightened up and stared at her.

Like a summons: something he had always known would come again. A cold thrill, that his oh-so practical life could be perpetually linked with something so infuriatingly and gloriously unpredictable. And always it would be disruptive and bring chaos in its wake. And this time there were things that he did not want to be hurt. But as always, his deepest, most secret reaction was: at last.

He turned back and looked at the apple tree. 'I wonder how high it'll get,' he said.

She pressed his arm again. 'Who's the Doctor, Alastair?'

'Yes, we met Peter Warmsly,' said the Doctor, putting down his third glass of water. 'He seems very knowledgeable.'

Shou Yuing helped herself to more of Ace's crisps. 'That's one way of putting it. He has a thing about King Arthur. Digs things out of the ground by the lake. You'd think he was living the legend.'

'He is an archaeologist,' said the Doctor.

The Chinese girl sighed. 'I can't see it myself. All that patient scraping. I keep getting the urge to bung half a kilo of TNT down a hole and bring the lot up in one go.'

'Now you're talking,' enthused Ace.

The Doctor glanced at his eager companion in annoyance. Despite all he had shown her, she still refused to learn respect for Time's disparate patterns. 'The point of archaelogy is to carefully recover the past. Not disintegrate it.'

'It won't make any difference,' said Shou Yuing. 'The only half decent thing Peter ever found is that.' She pointed up above the fireplace to where a blackened scabbard hung.

The Doctor walked across the room from the bar and stared up at the battered relic.

Ace nudged Shou Yuing and whispered. 'You could try something with more brisence.'

'More brisence than tri-nitro-toluene? Like what?'

Ace tapped her rucksack. 'Tell you outside. He gets upset when I talk about explosives.'

They slipped out of the garden door, leaving the Doctor engrossed in the scabbard. Its antiquity was strangely familiar − like deja-vu approached from the wrong end. Perhaps it would one day become familiar. But that was the random pattern of Time he had been trying to explain to Ace.

'Interesting, isn't it?' said Elizabeth Rowlinson.

'Yes,' he said. She had been sitting so quietly in the warm sunshine that he had almost forgotten her. She smiled, but did not move her head towards him. Her fingers left the pages of the Braille book she had been reading. 'Sometimes I can feel its presence. Silly, of course.'

Without even consulting his copy of Malory, he said, 'The scabbard is worth ten of the sword.'

'Touch it.'

He reached out cautiously and pulled away his hand fast. 'It's hot.'

At a second attempt, the scabbard was cold as stone.

Elizabeth nodded. 'Sometimes I get the strangest feeling about it.'

'What sort of feeling?'

'I can hear its quietness. It's as if it's waiting for something.'

'Something?' the Doctor muttered. 'Or someone.'

A car pulled abruptly to a halt outside and a door slammed. Peter Warmsly burst into the lounge.

'Elizabeth, I need to use your phone. The one in my car's not working.'

'Doctor Warmsly,' said the Doctor. 'Just the man I've been looking for.'

Peter was already barking a number down the telephone at the electronic operator. He turned round and seeing the Doctor, snapped, 'They've driven a bloody great rocket on to my land. My land!' He slammed down the receiver and swore. 'The line's dead!'

'I'm sorry, Peter, it must be the storm,' said Elizabeth.

'About this scabbard,' butted in the Doctor. 'Where was it found?'

Peter's mind was elsewhere. 'What are you saying?'

'The scabbard.' The Doctor began to unhitch the relic from the wall. 'Do you remember where it was found?'

'Careful with that?' He lifted the scabbard away from the Doctor and cradled it protectively. ' "The scabbard's worth . . ." '

' "... worth ten of the sword," said Merlin,' chorused the Doctor.

'I found it at the dig by the lake.'

'What period?'

'Eighth century AD.'

The Doctor shook his head. 'No, that can't be right.'

Peter curbed his temper. 'Excuse me Doctor, but getting that rocket off Trust land is a bit more important. The whole place is crawling with soldiers.'

'No, the scabbard's been waiting around longer than that.' The Doctor looked through the window at the sunlit garden. Smashed trees and the empty sky above.

'Waiting? Waiting for who?' said Peter.

Smashed trees below and figures like ants in the confines of her crystal sphere. Seen from on high, as the world looks from a window in the High Tagel.

'Waiting for me.'

The Black Knight waited until the two grey hunters had passed on the false trail. He had recognized Sir Comus and Sir Madlamor immediately. Both knights from Morgaine's closest retinue; cronies of the ruffian Prince Mordred. And somewhere there was a third, the leader of the sortie.

He started to retrace his steps back to the road. Through his helmet's receiver, he caught snatches of localized transmissions. Flashes of thought in the ether, but whether they were the spells and incantations of this world or glimpses of angels, this lowly knight had not the wit to understand them. But he could seek out someone who might.

He stepped out onto the path and the tree beside him exploded in flame.

The hunters had doubled back as well. Shots exploded round him as he ducked into the cover of the smoke.

He placed himself behind a fallen branch and waited, gun in hand. The Grey Knights were calling out ahead of him and another surly voice answered them from behind. The sortie leader at last.

'Do you have him?'

'Yes, my lord. Pinned down yonder between us.'

The Black Knight rose to make a run, but another blast of fire scored across his flank. He crouched down again, feeling the heat of the blast through his armour.

Already his suit assessed the course of action. Its umberere screen scripted out a clear route to the left. He turned to run, but a movement in the bushes caught his attention. A metal-grey capsule clattered at his feet.

A firecone. No runner was swift enough to clear its scatter zone.

Only one course was open. With his armour only half-powered for the leap, he leapt. The blast caught him just hands high in the air and flung him into the sky like a projectile from a ballista.

Shou Yuing couldn't fathom Ace out. The teenager defied all attempts at social stereotype categorizing that Shou Yuing's amateur psychology could throw up. The clothes and the attitude were all wrong. The vernacular was bizzare. This one has problems, she thought, and liked Ace even better.

They pulled up a couple of overturned chairs and sat with their drinks at a damp garden table.

Ace never stopped talking. She treated Shou Yuing as a soul mate who she hadn't seen for years. But if she and the Doctor had been travelling for a long time, then that could be a lonely business. Her eagerness reminded Shou Yuing of her own brother, except that where he was into motorbikes, Ace was into explosives. And it was clear that she was no innocent on the subject either.

Out of her bag, Ace produced two canisters of something called nitro-nine. Shou Yuing would have laughed it off, but she and her brother had helped out on the local Guy Fawkes night displays. The fireworks there were supervized by experts, but Shou Yuing could tell just by sense of smell that these little bombshells were twice as potent and real.

Ace could only be categorized as an embryonic anarchist, yet Shou Yuing was certain there was not an ounce of malice in her.

'I started with homemade jelly,' Ace said. 'That's gelignite. I used to put it together in the art lessons, right?'

'Right.' Shou Yuing giggled warily.

'So Mrs Parkinson, the art teacher, catches me and asks what it is. So I told her it was plasticine. Well, I couldn't tell her what it really was ...'

'The gelignite ...'

'That's right. So we're in the corridor by now, and she tells me to put what she thinks is plasticine back in the art room.'

Shou Yuing was revelling in this story even though she could see exactly where it was going. 'So what did you do?'

'I chucked it over my shoulder.' Ace screwed up the crisp packet and threw it. 'Like that! It landed right in the middle of 1C's prizewinning pottery pig collection and,' she flung her arms wide, '. . . boom!'

The sky momentarily flickered white towards the lake.

'Boom?' shouted Shou Yuing.

'Boom!' yelled the anarchist.

The distant crump of an explosion rattled the windows of the hotel. Ace and Shou Yuing stared at the sky as something like a suit of armour whistled overhead and hit the roof of Pat Rowlinson's brewery.

'I'd better get the Doctor,' shouted Ace.

The door opened. 'Good idea,' said the Doctor as he stepped outside. 'Did you see it?'

'Yes,' they chorused.

'And?'

'It looked like a man,' said Ace.

The Doctor frowned. 'A man flying through the air?'

'And then through the roof,' added Shou Yuing.

He regarded the brewery roof where it was punctured by a large hole. 'I think you should stay here,' he said, setting off.

'Be serious, Professor,' yelled Ace.

Shou Yuing grabbed at her arm. 'What's going on?'

'The business.' Ace started to run after the Doctor, who had already reached the brewery. 'You'll have to ask the Professor.'

They caught up with the Doctor as he leaned an ear against the wooden door.

'What's going on?' insisted Shou Yuing.

The Doctor shushed her and slowly pushed the door inwards. Inside, he grappled about in the dark and finally found a switch.

Cold fluorescence lit the tall fermentation vats. A haze of dust was still settling on the bricks and broken tiles that littered the floor. The place reeked of beer.

One of the vats was dented. At its foot lay a figure in black armour, his suit battered and the mirrorshade visor cracked.

The suit's arm rose weakly and fell back again. A man's voice groaned and muttered, 'Excalibur. Darkness must not prevail.'

'Is it an android?' asked Ace.

Shou Yuing stared at Ace and the Doctor and then back at the broken figure. This was crazy. These two weirdos were behaving as if this was an everyday occurrence. Who the hell were they? She forgot that she had promised to be back home by teatime.

The Doctor knelt by the knight. 'No Ace, it's a man in powered armour.' He felt around the edges of the helmet, found the clips and pulled it away.

The Black Knight looked up at them with ice blue eyes. Long yellow hair framed his classically handsome features.

'Oh, very Teutonic,' observed the Doctor. 'How do you do? This is Ace and I am...'

'Merlin!' cried the Black Knight. His smile broadened in wonder and recognition. 'Merlin, against all hope!'

Part 2

Scenario: Broken Arrow

'...Merlin, who knew the range of all their arts,
Had built the King his havens, ships and halls,
Was also Bard, and knew the starry heavens...

'The Idylls of the King'
Tennyson

Chapter 1

Doris watched the helicopter settle on the lawn like a malevolent black insect. The trees and plants quailed under the surge of its propwash.

She turned and re-entered the house where Alastair was finalizing arrangements. She thought that his Brigadier's uniform looked a little tight, but there was a rightness to it. For all his acquired domesticity, the man of action still lived on underneath. She reprimanded herself for being flustered, while he, who was going off to face heaven knows what, maintained an outward appearance of complete composure.

The cup of coffee with which she always finished lunch was stone cold. The food was hardly picked at.

He had finished his.

She tried to imagine the magnitude of crisis that could summon him out of retirement. Worse, she was sure that he was eager to go.

There had been a night when his restless sleep had woken her. She had heard him mutter: 'Corporal Bell. Chap with the wings. Five rounds rapid.' And then he grabbed her arm and yelled: 'Doctor! Don't do it!'

Although names like Mike Yates and Sarah-Jane Smith occasionally cropped up in conversation, the true nature of his military career was kept a closely guarded secret. She respected him too much to ask about it.

She had gleaned information from other sources, notably the *State Secret* TV documentary, but the Doctor had never been mentioned at all.

'What do you think?' Lethbridge-Stewart asked. 'I'd worried it wouldn't fit me. But not bad, eh?'

'Alastair,' she said. She had kept his UNIT cap badge hidden in some vague hope that it might delay his departure. But there was no point. It was better to wave him bravely and dutifully off. She pressed the badge into his hand. 'Alastair, I found this.'

He smiled and pinned it on to his cap. 'Thank you.'

One final glance at the mirror. 'Well, I'd better be off then,' he said. She handed him his case and followed him out into the garden. He gave a wave of acknowledgement to the pilot who waited in the helicopter. The propwash blew Doris's auburn hair into disarray.

'You will be careful, won't you?'

'I've always been careful. Don't worry, I'll sort this out and come home.' He held her tightly and she kissed him on the cheek. Then she pulled away.

'I think they're waiting for you,' she said quickly.

'Of course.'

The Brigadier straightened up. She watched him walk briskly towards the helicopter and climb in next to the pilot.

The machine tilted forward slightly as it lifted away. Doris saw him give a brief wave and she raised her hand in response. The helicopter was already disappearing over the trees. Away north towards East Grinstead and London beyond.

Why wasn't Alastair too old for this? Too comfortable and retired. Surely they could have found someone else. She thought that if he didn't come back, her heart would break.

'Merlin!' exclaimed Shou Yuing.

'You've got it wrong, mate, this is the Doctor,' insisted Ace.

The Black Knight was laughing as he pulled at the buckles of the jesseraunte armour. He met the Doctor's stare head on. 'Oh, he has many names, but in my reckoning he is Merlin.'

The Doctor helped prise the dead armour open, allowing the knight to move freely. Underneath, he wore a hauberk of light chain mail.

Testing the armour in his hands for its strength and composition, the Doctor said casually, 'So you recognized my face then?'

'No. It's not your aspect, but your manner that betrays you.'

The Doctor raised an eyebrow.

'Do you not ride the ship of Time?' went on the knight. 'Does it not deceive the senses, being smaller without than within? Merlin, cease these games and tell me truly. Is this the time?'

'The time for what?'

The knight was apparently perplexed. 'Thou dost not know, truly?'

Ace's patience finally ran out. 'Do you think he'd be asking if he did, tinhead?'

Instantly, the young man drew his sword and raised the blade in an earnest salute. 'Why, the answer to Excalibur's call,' he cried. 'The time of retribution. The time when Arthur rises to lead the Britons to war!'

'Vortigern's Lake,' muttered the Doctor. He ignored Ace's quizzical look and studied the young knight. The tribes of the chieftain Arthur's Dark Ages were a wild and generally untrained group of freedom fighters, a world away from this warrior. He resembled a fragment of romanticized legend, yet his ideals and objectives were all too real and dangerous. There had never been anything like this knight on the real Earth — at least not on any Earth the Doctor knew.

'Can you walk?' he asked.

'Aye,' said the knight eagerly, and sheathed his sword again.

Shou Yuing was beginning to be reminded of a local pageant. 'Would someone please tell me what is going on?' she complained.

The Doctor wished he knew. The answer was, it appeared, a world away — and then he guessed. 'If my hunch is correct, the Earth could be at the centre of a war that doesn't even belong in this dimension.'

Ace threw Shou Yuing a look of sympathy. She knew what it was like trying to keep up with the Doctor.

The brewery door crashed open and a figure in UNIT

uniform, holding a hi-tech rifle like a machine gun, burst in on them.

'Everybody stand nice and easy,' ordered Brigadier Bambera.

How very tiresome, thought the Doctor. 'Excuse me, Winifred,' he said, 'but we have to be somewhere urgently. So if you could just let us get past.'

She focused the gun directly on him. 'You're under arrest, you and your freaky friends!'

'Who are you calling freaky?' shouted Ace.

The Doctor deliberately pushed Ace behind him out of the firing line and added, 'I'm sure we can sort this out quite quickly. If I could just explain...'

A loud fizz behind them like a firecracker, dissolved a section of the brewery wall into smoke. Three figures in grey armour stood in the gap carrying heavy-duty guns that resembled sawn-off lances.

'Take them,' shouted the leader.

To the Doctor's dismay, Bambera automatically trained her gun on the newcomers and yelled, 'I am an armed military officer and you are under arrest! Lay down your weapons and put your hands in the air!'

'Winifred, that is not the right approach,' protested the Doctor.

'Put the guns down!' she shouted. The Black Knight tensed and his hand went to his sword. Shou Yuing edged backwards behind a vat. The three figures advanced.

Ace saw the Doctor step directly into the knights' path. She reached for her nitro-nine and found she had left her knapsack in the garden.

'Well, now that we're all here, let me introduce myself. I'm the Doctor and this is...'

The Grey leader levelled his gun, but Bambera released a volley of shots directly at his head. He fell back against his companions, his mirrored visor cracked across.

The Black Knight launched himself at Bambera, knocking her to the floor as the wall behind them disappeared in a burst of splintered brick. 'One favour returned, my lady,' he said in her ear. He turned and saw his fallen sword lying across the floor out of reach.

A pair of small hands grasped the massive hilt and tried to drag up the broadsword.

'Ace! No!' hissed the Doctor from cover.

The Grey leader had recovered and was advancing towards the Black Knight and Bambera with his gun raised. 'Mine,' he said and his minions waited.

Hardly able to lift the huge sword, Ace stepped out and swung the weapon at the Grey leader's legs. He tripped and hit the floor, his visor shattering. His gun skittered away across the tiles.

Bambera had struggled out from under the Black Knight. She clambered to her feet and brought her gun to bear on the Grey leader.

'All right, you want to try that again?' she said.

Bits of visor fell from the leader's helmet as he struggled to his feet. He waved back his advancing men and ripped off the remains of the helmet to reveal his handsome saturnine features.

'Mordred!' exclaimed the Black Knight.

The prince nodded. 'Ancelyn ap Gwalchmai. How fitting that you should die amongst peasants.'

'Look again, Mordred,' said Ancelyn and glanced meaning-fully at the Doctor, who was emerging from behind the vat.

'Remember me?' said the Doctor hopefully and raised his hat.

Mordred stared for a moment, and then his eyes widened in angry recognition. These were the mocking tones that had plagued his thoughts so often over a thousand years or more. 'Merlin!'

'Not again!' moaned Ace.

'You were bound!' accused the prince. 'My mother sealed you into the ice caves for all eternity.'

The Doctor sneered. 'I am the master of time. I am not bound so easily.'

'Master of lies!'

Ancelyn levelled his sword at Mordred's chest. 'Beware your tongue, Mordred. Have you so easily forgotten Badon, where he cast down your mother with his mighty arts?'

'Yes,' insisted the Doctor fiercely, 'remember Badon and my

mighty arts!' He was rather enjoying this verbal joust with the
undefinable and added, 'Do you think I would use mere trickery
against one as formidable as you? Now go, before I unleash
a terrible...' he reached to conjure some elemental force from
the air, '...a terrible something upon you!'

'Go, Mordred, while you still live,' warned Ancelyn.

Mordred's eyes narrowed with hatred. 'There will be a
reckoning, Ancelyn. I promise it. And as for you, mighty wizard
Merlin, my mother Morgaine has waited twelve centuries to
face you. You will bow down before her this time.'

He turned and led his knights away through the gap.

Ace pressed her hand on the Doctor's arm. 'Who was that?'

He sniffed dismissively and watched the knights as they
disappeared into the woods. 'That was Mordred,' he said
knowledgeably. 'And his mother is Morgaine, a mighty
sorceress.'

'You know these guys then?' asked Shou Yuing, who had
finally emerged from hiding.

The Doctor shook his head. 'Never seen them before.'

Ancelyn began to gather up his armour. Its last duty had been
to shield him from the energies of the firecone's explosion and
break his fall. Then it was dead and its visor cracked across.
He could no longer leap from Avallion back to the world.

It had been his armour since his knighting, embossed with
the emblems of fights and favours he had won. He stacked its
cold, chitinous sections with fond care, remembering the origin
of each scratch and chink. But he was no longer alone. Where
Merlin was, so would Arthur be.

'Winifred. A word,' said the Doctor, 'and in comfort please.
I suspect it's my round again.' He was out of the brewery and
heading back to the hotel before Bambera could argue.

'Come on, Sir Galahad,' said Ace.

Ancelyn fixed her with a grave smile. 'Not so, damosel. Sir
Galahad of blessed memory was the grandest great-grandfather
of my great-grandfather's great great grand-uncle, and a solemn
holy knight.'

'Sorry,' said Ace. Families were other people's problem −
a fact she repeated to herself with worrying regularity.

Ancelyn slapped her merrily on the back. 'No matter. My parage is tangled as a briar patch. You need a stick to unpick the thicket.' He paused, apparently waiting for a response.

Ace glanced at Shou Yuing. 'I wish he'd let us in on the joke,' she muttered.

'I think he just has,' confessed Shou Yuing. But she grinned because her grandmother had always told such tales of their family's ancestors. The tales were in Mandarin; in fifty-three years as a British subject, Granny had not learned one word of English.

The young women hurried after the Doctor, leaving Ancelyn and Bambera to follow.

They collided in the door.

'I want to talk to you,' said the brigadier.

One corner of the knight's mouth sidled into a mischievous grin. 'I am Ancelyn ap Gwalchmai, the Sperhawk. Knight General of the Britons. I do not talk to peasants.'

Frustrations that had been smouldering since the early hours finally ignited. Bambera raised her fist, Ancelyn caught it and they fell through the open door in a tangle on to the muddy path and lawn.

Ace glanced back and saw the fight in progress. 'Professor!'

There was a cry of pain from one of the grappling protagonists.

'Don't worry about them,' advised the Doctor without even looking. 'They're just establishing their credentials.'

'They've got a funny way of doing it.' Ace stared back at the fracas. At the moment, Bambera seemed to be getting the better of the knight. But he seemed to be laughing.

'What should we worry about then?' asked Shou Yuing.

'Sorcery,' said the Doctor and hurried into the hotel.

Night slipped across the surface of the sky like a film of oily darkness. It spread not from the east, but from an apex directly over the decaying priory close to the Tarchester road. Above the broken timbers of the roof, the stars were stifled.

In a pool of their own unnatural glare stood two orbs on tripods of ancient iron. Mordred set his sword between them and knelt on the stone flags. He felt the source of his own power grow closer and spoke its words in the stillness.

'Here is the convocation. This is the place of meeting. The point between two worlds, two universes, two realities.'

Like a traced line of gunpowder, an octogrammaton burned its pattern across the floor before him. The air turned sickly and sulphurous.

He grasped his sword and slowly raised it above his head. 'By this sword, brother to Excalibur, I part the curtain of night.'

'Nobody is to go outside,' said the Doctor. He stood by the hotel bar and lectured his astonished audience.

Elizabeth Rowlinson sat stock-still on the settee gripping her husband's hand. 'I heard gunshots,' she said.

'Exactly,' said the Doctor.

Pat Rowlinson was not a demonstrative man, but there were limits and his hotel was full of mad people. He wanted to close up early. 'What is this, Doctor? You can't just walk in here and impose siege conditions...'

The Doctor tutted at him irritably. 'Did you see how quickly darkness fell? There are things out there in the night that you don't want to meet.'

'What things?' scoffed Peter Warmsly. He was not paying tonight and was already on his third pint.

The garden door banged shut. Ancelyn, his hands cuffed in front of him, was pushed into the room by Winifred Bambera. She held up her UNIT ID and announced her rank.

The Doctor looked in surprise at Ancelyn. 'What happened to you?'

The knight slumped down into a chair and cheerfully showed off his bonds. 'She vanquished me, and I threw myself on her mercy!'

Distant thunder rolled and Elizabeth tensed.

Bambera ignored Ancelyn's grin and went on with her routine. The situation made it doubly important. 'As of now I am in charge here. Everyone remain calm and we'll soon have everything under control.'

'I doubt it,' said the Doctor. 'It all depends on what Mordred has in mind.'

Peter had been staring in astonishment at Ancelyn. 'Mordred?' he said in total disbelief. As an archaeologist, he restricted his fantasies to dreams. He had never considered his reaction should they walk up to him in a hotel bar.

He was suddenly aware that no one was speaking. Everyone was staring across the room at the ancient scabbard. It rattled in its mounting above the fireplace, apparently trying to tear itself in a frenzy away from the wall.

There was a flash of lightning not necessarily outside the room. The scabbard flung itself off the wall in a shower of plaster. It travelled across the room like a spear and embedded itself in the panelled wall inches from Peter's head.

Thunder boomed and the glasses on shelves behind the bar began to launch themselves over the edge like lemmings.

Peter's tankard dribbled beer as it cracked and finally shattered in his hand.

The walls of the hotel shuddered. Ace and Shou Yuing burst in from the hallway yelling.

'What's happening?' shouted Bambera.

They all looked at the Doctor. The Doctor looked at Ancelyn.

'She is coming,' said the knight.

'Across the abyss, life calls to life, biomass to biomass, energy to energy. To Avallion I summon thee from beyond the confines of this universe.'

Plumes of energy spiralled like snakes along the blade of Mordred's raised sword. Lightning played among the bare timbers of the priory roof. It cracked between the two light rippled orbs.

The prince yelled and plunged the steel blade into the flagstones with a shower of sparks. The grinding mechanics of two cosmoses in spiralling collision began to grate out of the air. The octogrammaton before him surged with light like the furnace of a dragon's heart.

As a child delights in playing with fire, so Mordred played with natural energies, the science of magic. The flames of Creation were summoned and focused between the two orbs.

Bound to his will, the forces coalesced and ripped a hole in the fabric of existence. A burning wind blew into his face. He clung to the hilt of his sword and stared into the gaping abyss between realities. Lit by the harsh glare of his power, he began to laugh with elation. His summons was a hand that reached in need from one world to another. As light calls to darkness, as hunger calls to greed, and as a boy calls to his mother.

'Who's She?' said Ace.

Thunder, or worse than thunder, rumbled outside the hotel. The Doctor fingered the trembling scabbard as he listened to Ancelyn's words.

'She holds the thirteen worlds under her yoke. Twelve centuries has she held them to her avail. It's true the lands are fruitful. The fields and champaigns spill with grain and fruit, but by dread is that earned. For she won the crown by her black arts and by those arts she has secured her power. Her worlds are built on the pretence of plenty, but they are stacked upon a foundation of darkness and evil.

'And those she rules, she milks through tributes and tailles. Her subjects, for all their wealth and righteousness, lived in that same dread. They are slaves to their queen.

'She is Morgaine, the immortal one. She who brought ruin to Arthur the High King. It is she whom Merlin opposes. And it is his summons through Excalibur that I answer.'

The Doctor touched the scabbard again; it was icy cold. 'But now Morgaine follows you, Ancelyn,' he said. 'For she fears that Merlin will fulfil the final prophesy. And then the High King will rise again and cast her into the abyss forever.'

'Yes, Merlin,' said Ancelyn.

'I thought so. She must be desperate.' The Doctor tried to focus down the length of the scabbard. He felt the strands of time beginning to fray under the assult of mighty power. 'Which way does this wall face?' he said.

'What's that got to do with it?' exclaimed Pat Rowlinson. 'What's happening?'

'It faces north,' said Elizabeth quietly. 'Towards the lake.'

The hotel shuddered under a fresh onslaught of elemental fury.

Above it all came a great rending sound, a tearing asunder of the veil of Eternity, the clamorous opening of the gates of hell.

The Doctor, pale as a corpse, fell forward to the floor in a swoon.

Alone in Doctor Warmsley's cottage, the wolfhound Cerberus trembled and yelped beneath the security of his master's bed.

Deep in the cavernous halls of the ship, the sword changed the notes of its signal. Beside it, the armoured figure that lay on the bier remained unmoving.

In the comfort of the warm helicopter, Brigadier Lethbridge-Stewart woke from his nap with a start. The lights of London moved below him and an inky pall of night spread across the dusky sky from the west. He felt a sudden chill of anxiety and shuddered.

Mordred saw a shape moving in the white depths of the rent between existences. It took on human form as it grew larger. The Prince bowed his head as the female figure stood silhouetted against the light.

'Immortal Morgaine. Ageless and Deathless.'

She stepped through the rent on to the stone of Avallion. Crowned and armoured with gold, she raised her head and drank in the air. Behind her, a dozen men-at-arms emerged from the light and took up positions of honour to their Queen.

Morgaine lifted her crown away with slender fingers and shook out her long red-gold hair, the mark of the seer.

'Mordred,' she said, her voice charged with ice.

He lifted his head. 'Mother. Merlin is here.'

'Yes, I can feel his presence.' She maintained the calm that always unnerved him. It meant that she was angry.

'And he has a new countenance.'

Morgaine smiled. 'Oh, he has worn many faces.' She stared up into the dark air beyond the bones of the roof. He had issued his challenge to her, so she must respond.

Merlin, she thought. Hear me now!

Humans dwell too much in the past; their extent of vision rarely spreads beyond the present. But that is an occupational hazard for any species that lives within the constrictions of time's passage. Happy the creature that can remember the future. The Doctor wished that he was blessed with such facility, if only to avoid the paradoxical confusion of being accused of some act he had yet to perpetrate.

He lay semi-conscious on the carpet, trying to clear his head of temporal disturbances and human witterings.

Merlin. Hear me now!

A voice in the darkness of his head. Not a moment's peace, he thought. A woman's voice, cold and domineering. 'I can hear you, Morgaine,' he said out loud.

Do not stand against me this time, Merlin. For your soul's sake.

The Doctor sat up oblivious of the concerned faces that surrounded him. 'I cannot allow your interference,' he said.

And he could see her now. A proud and regal warrior armoured in gold, lit by torchlight. She raised her hand aggressively and made a fist. *Then let this be our last battlefield!*

The thunder roared. She was gone. The torchlight in his head and the lights in the hotel bar blacked out simultaneously.

His human companions screamed.

Chapter 2

Pilot Lieutenant Françoise Lavel sat and waited in the warmth of her helicopter. The early morning air was crisp and clear over the river. After the storm rescue operations of the previous day, Thames Barrier Heliport was deceptively quiet. Lavel watched the freight barges that had rid the roads of innumerable lorries moving on the water.

'What's he like then? Over,' said the familiar voice at Docklands ATC.

'A bit crusty,' said Lavel. 'L'ecole antique, you know? But he's not as old as I'd thought he'd be. Over.'

'And does he live up to the legend? Over.'

A black saloon car was moving across the tarmac towards the helicopter.

'Can't talk now, ATC. Here he is. Over.'

'Roger Valkyrie 7. You have clearance from London Central. In your own time. Have fun with *la grande fromage*. Over and out.'

He's getting cheeky, thought Lavel to herself in English. She opened the passenger door and Brigadier Lethbridge-Stewart climbed into the cockpit.

'Morning, Lavel.'

'Good morning, sir.' She started to run the rotors up to speed.

As he fiddled with his safety belt, she noticed that he had cut himself shaving.

The helicopter rose from the pad and took its flight due west over central London. The buildings cast long shadows in the dawn light. The Brigadier stared down at the toy landscape, remembering action he had seen around St Paul's, Fleet Street and Covent Garden.

'How did it go, sir?' asked Lavel.

'What's that?'

'The briefing, sir.'

'Oh. Usual bureaucracy. Inch-thick forms and about half a pint of blood.' He returned to the view. The river beside Stanbridge House Conference Centre was a smooth grey, its surface undisturbed by anything larger than a single speedboat.

The briefing had gone better than he had imagined. Within reason he had been given carte blanche with available resources.

He had requested a two-kilometre exclusion zone around the convoy outside the limit of radio jamming. The area just cleared the edge of Carbury village. With the bulk of European UNIT handling the Azanian ceasefire, the Czech engineering group had been spared from flood relief in the low countries. They were being flown into the DOZ that morning.

'Funny how even London looks beautiful at sunrise.'

'I never noticed, sir. Seen one heliport and you've seen them all.' She punched up the Mapscan on her Japanese monitor. 'Straight to Carbury, sir?'

'That's right,' he said with a look of satisfied anticipation. 'Where the action is.'

Lavel punched in the village name. The monitor presented a one inch to the klick ordnance map of Cornwall.

The Brigadier flicked through information on the screen of his portable operations desk. 'Any word from Major Husak yet?'

Lavel shook her head. 'No, sir. And London says that the area of radio interference is expanding. No contact now for thirteen hours. And with that second storm last night ...'

'Yes, quite. We'll try raising them when we get closer. Do you speak Czech?'

She grinned. 'Only when I'm drunk, sir.'

He smiled and scrolled the information. The latest jargon took some getting used to. 'The Brigadier who's baby-sitting the missile. Bambera?'

'Yes, sir. Bambera.'

'Hmm ... sounds African. Good man, is he?'

Lavel bit her tongue.

From the wooded hill over the village, the Doctor saw a squad of UNIT jeeps heading towards the lake.

He had been reading his copy of Malory by the first pale light of the morning, until the dawn chorus made it impossible to concentrate.

Through the garden, he followed a trail of broken furniture. Piece by piece, he picked up Ancelyn's sword, Bambera's automatic and her beret. He was grateful to see that Ace had retrieved the sack of nitro-nine that she assumed he knew nothing about.

In the darkened bar, he found Ancelyn still handcuffed and asleep on one of the wallseats. Beside him, Bambera had finally succumbed to sleep as well. Her head was resting on his shoulder. Again, the Doctor recalled that Winifred was a variation of Guenever, and doubtless Ancelyn was a direct descendant of Lancelot du Lac. He had just been reading of all the trouble that liaison had caused. Perhaps Arthur had needed all the help he could get.

The Doctor picked up one of Ace's discarded crisp bags, blew it up and smacked it between his hands.

The loud bang had Ancelyn and Bambera on their feet, back to back, glancing round for enemies.

'Good morning,' said the Doctor as he disappeared into the hall.

The sword, gun and beret were set out on a table with a note saying *If you must*.

A car horn sounded from the front of the hotel. Bambera scowled at Ancelyn and beat him through the door. By the time they had fought their way out to the front of the hotel, Peter Warmsly's car was heading up the drive with the shapes of the Doctor and Ace in the back. Shou Yuing's car was already gone.

'Doctor!' yelled Bambera.

'Such anger, my lady?'

74

'I want that man back!' She also wanted her convoy, her car and to know what was going on. She did not want to be stuck with this grinning idiot, who pretended to be a knight from a Hollywood epic.

Ancelyn nodded after the car. 'Merlin cannot be held. He makes the laws and goes where he will. It was always so. If we would speak with him, my lady, we needs must follow.'

Lifting his handcuffed arms towards her, he began to jog backwards up the drive. He was holding his sword.

She swore loudly, because she had nearly laughed. There was nothing for it; she set off up the drive after him.

There was no sign of Morgaine or her forces as they drove towards the lake. The Doctor was quiet, which Ace recognized as determination. But if he was mighty wizard Merlin, what did that make her? His familiar? Certainly no one knew as much about him as she did. Except it never seemed to work out that way.

Peter Warmsly was keen to show off the Carbury dig to the Doctor. But he never mentioned the previous night's events. Ace wondered if he could cope with them.

He parked the car beside the lake and eyed the soldiers across the tape barriers surrounding the missile convoy.

Fresh troops seemed to have arrived bringing fresh activity with them. The Doctor gave them a sidelong glance, but put up a good show of being more interested in Peter's work.

'So you excavated all this by yourself,' he said. 'Very impressive.'

The site looked like a set of muddy squares to Ace. Peter skirted the edges of them and enthused, 'Well, it was something of a labour of love. And lately I've had Shou Yuing to help.'

The Doctor peered at the mud as if he could read it like a book. 'Where did you find the scabbard?'

Peter pointed to a red marker pennant and started walking towards it.

'How long has it taken?' called Ace.

'About ten years.'

The Doctor nudged her. 'Archaeology is a delicate and precise

75

skill. History has to be eased out of the earth one painstaking layer at a time.'

'Yeah, but ten years digging with a dustpan and brush ...' She looked down at the flat area of stone she was standing on. It was covered in weather-worn runes. 'What's this?'

'Ah, that's a bit of a mystery,' said Peter. 'I've had experts from everywhere to look at it, but no one can decipher the carvings.'

The Doctor frowned at the runes and then looked away across the lake. 'It says *Dig Hole Here*,' he said.

Peter was astonished. 'Extraordinary. What does it say that in?'

'My handwriting.'

Never mind that the script was Ancient Gallifreyan, this was the final proof that he hadn't particularly wanted to find. He had obviously been here in the past, somebody's past, but it certainly wasn't his.

So much for archaeology. 'Ace! I need a hole here.'

'Right,' she said and pulled out a canister of nitro-nine that they both knew he did/didn't know about. 'How long?'

'Sixty seconds should be enough.'

She turned the tiny dial on the lid and planted the canister beside the rune stone.

Peter looked alarmed as the Doctor started to lead him clear. 'Long enough for what?'

'This way please. There's nothing to worry about, my young friend is something of an expert.'

'In archaeology?' said Peter as Ace hurriedly took his other arm.

'No. Explosives,' said the Doctor.

'What!'

A blast of a brisence far greater than either the Doctor or Ace had expected hurled the three of them into the ditch for which they had been heading.

They lay face down in the mud while more hot earth showered down on them. The shouts of the soldiers could be heard. Peter Warmsly was speechless.

'I think the timer needs more work,' said Ace.

The Doctor shook earth out of his hat. 'One day, Ace, we are going to have a long talk about acceptable safety standards.'

He climbed out of the ditch and walked at speed back to what was left of the dig. Ace ran after him. He jumped and vanished into the smoking crater. It was at least four metres across and three deep. Not bad.

Ace looked back and saw Peter yelling at the soldiers. In shock, he was ordering them off Trust land.

'What's down there?' she called to the Doctor.

He was poking at the crater wall with his umbrella. She heard a tumble of stones through the smoke and heard him say, 'Aha. It's a tunnel.'

'A dark mysterious one?'

'Probably.'

'Leading to unknown dangers?'

'Oh, certainly.'

'Wicked!' She vaulted to the bottom in one go as Peter Warmsly came puffing up to the crater's edge.

'Vandals!' he shouted. 'I've been excavating this site for ten years!'

The smoke cleared and the Doctor saw his crimson face glaring down at him. 'Peter,' he said with extraordinary calmness and authority, 'Ace and I are going to investigate the tunnel. I want you to guard this end. No one is to come down here. No one.'

'Oh yes, I'll give them a lecture on archaeology!'

'Good idea. We'll bring you something back.'

He quickly ushered Ace through the dark gap in the wall. They were inside a low tubular tunnel which smelt of fish. The only light trickled in from the gap behind them. They had to stoop to walk.

'It's damp,' said Ace and her voice echoed into the distance.

'Yes. It leads under the lake.'

She touched the tunnel sides. 'This wall's made of concrete.'

The Doctor scraped the surface with a Victorian fruit knife that he always used as a spatula. 'It's gone soft with age. It must have been put up in the eighth century.'

'They didn't have concrete in those days.'

'No, they didn't.'

'Thought so.'

He couldn't see her knowing grin in the dim light, but he knew it was there. There was a heavy sliding crunch behind them. The way out vanished. The tunnel pitched into darkness.

'Doctor!' She stood up and her head hit the ceiling.

'Don't worry Ace, it's just a trap,' said his voice, right by her ear.

She could hear water dripping further on, but she could not move. The clinging darkness was choking her.

She felt his hand on her arm. Slowly he began to lead her towards heaven knows what.

Lavel circled the helicopter over Carbury.

Radio contact with the Czech group under Major Husak had been lost as soon as the squad entered the area. Triangulation pinpointed the source of interference as Vortigern's Lake to the north of the village. The Brigadier naturally expected to find the Doctor somewhere close to the source of the trouble. But he wanted a thorough recce of the village first. He knew from bitter experience that if the Doctor was on form, no one would ever find out what was going on until it was all over.

There was plenty of storm damage around Carbury and the single road through the village was deserted. He scoured the landscape below for something familiar, preferably an abandoned police box. There was nothing.

Despite seeing one roadblock set up on the village perimeter, the Brigadier was unsure that the exclusion zone was working. He was not even certain that he would recognize the Doctor when he did run into him.

He saw a glint of metal coming from the direction of the Norman church and half glimpsed a row of soldiers formed up through the trees.

'Take her round again, Lavel,' he said. Something niggled at the back of his mind. 'Are you armed, Lieutenant?'

'Yes, sir.'

'Check it's loaded in case we go in.'

The helicopter started its turn back towards the church.

Morgaine stood beside her son in a strange world. Her personal entourage of men-at-arms was arrayed in readiness beside her. They watched the pale sky beyond the stone tower.

'What did you see?' she said to Mordred.

'A flying machine. Like an ornithopter but with whirling blades for wings.'

Avallion had been neglected for too long. It had ceased to be the haven that the ancient books of lore described. Morgaine had watched for an age, but she had not turned her eyes this way. Perhaps Avallion was no longer the dwelling place for peasants.

'The people of this world are obsessed with machinery,' she said.

'So it would seem,' said her son.

'And thus by default, they can have no love of the living. Nor bear honour for their fellows.'

The roar of the flying machine was growing louder again. It swooped in on them from behind the trees.

Morgaine gathered her power within her. 'Well then, let us teach them the limitations of their technologies.'

She flung out her arm and a bolt of electric blue light shot from her fingers.

A small explosion flamed from the rear of the flying machine's undercarriage.

Warning klaxons blared in the cockpit. The helicopter lurched to one side.

'Malfunction!' yelled Lavel. 'Port engine! Felt like we hit something! Strap in. This could be rough!'

Lethbridge-Stewart clung to his seat. The helicopter started to spiral, leaving a coil of black smoke in its wake.

'Can we get down?' he said.

Red hazard lights flickered across the panel. Lavel clung to the controls and tried to right the portward list. 'Down is not the problem,' she snapped.

Mordred and Morgaine watched the flying machine sink like a wounded bird until it vanished beyond the woodland. They heard the crash of wood against metal and glass. Smoke still rose in a drifting column.

She turned away and stared down at the cold damp earth. Her power was weaker here. In the world at home, she would have blasted the machine out of the sky.

Arthur had chosen their final meeting place well. He had lured her here, knowing full well of this flaw in her power. Or were these the tricks of that jealous fool Merlin, who held the High King's ear in every matter from battle strategy to the choicest table wine?

No matter. Arthur had fled in the face of defeat. It had taken him twelve hundred years to summon courage to return and face her. She had scoured the Thirteen Planets for clues to his whereabouts. He may have been engaged in some protracted war, or beleagured in some eternal siege; she dismissed out of hand the rumour that he was bound in sleep, waiting to rise again like some hero of legend.

More likely, he had been sulking somewhere, his mind turning sourer and sicker as he nurtured some malignant plot against her. The mind of an immortal was always hungry for fresh stimulation. Allowed to linger with its own dark thoughts, it soon shrivelled to single coursed obsessions and madness.

After so long, whatever scheme he hatched, she would still meet and confound his every ploy. The power was still hers. She reminded herself daily of the duplicity for which she had vowed he would pay.

'Before this battle is out, both Arthur and Merlin will rot in Hell!'

Let every spirit hear her decree. And so be it.

The helicopter lay burning in the undergrowth of a small copse. Its rotors were twisted and broken. Its cockpit window smashed.

As the Brigadier pulled Lavel clear of the craft, she grimaced and clutched at her leg. 'I'm all right!' she choked through gritted teeth.

He supported her as they struggled for cover. Behind them, the fuel tanks erupted into a giant fireball. Lethbridge-Stewart and Lavel hurled themselves forward into the bracken as a barrage of shrapnel scythed overhead.

He thought she was going to cry. 'Seven million quid's worth of aircraft and I lost it. If they make me pay for that, I'll be poor forever.'

The Brigadier fingered her leg and she winced. 'I think you've pulled a ligament,' he said awkwardly.

'Good! I thought it might be something serious.'

He stood up and looked round to get his bearings. The church tower reared through the trees beyond the burning helicopter. 'I'm going to get help from the village.'

She screwed up her eyes, because he was standing with the sun directly behind him. 'Sir, we don't know what the situation is yet.'

He drew his pistol, the gun he had always kept since the old days. They had offered him a new revomatic at London Central, but if he had to fight, he wanted to do it comfortably.

'The situation is normal and it doesn't get much worse than that.' He took a deep breath. 'Do you know, I think I'm beginning to enjoy this.'

He disappeared in the direction of the church leaving lavel alone in the warm damp grass.

The lieutenant immediately set about fashioning herself a makeshift crutch from one of her crashed helicopter's landing struts.

She tried her weight on the support. Her leg ached dully, but she was able to stand and drink in the sunlit air. It put her in mind of her home in Brittany; there was an atmosphere of something ancient and unfathomable that haunted both Cornish and Breton regions. The Celtic links were tangible in both history and myth. She loosened her tightly-pinned hair and shook it free. Somewhere, a lark rose singing into the blue-white sky.

Lavel was suddenly aware of someone approaching through the copse.

Pat Rowlinson, a first-aid kit under his arm, had come searching for survivors from the crash. He stopped to stare at the smoking shell of the helicopter and tensed as he felt the cold metal of a gun press in by his ear.

'Don't move,' said Lavel. 'Where are you from?'

He managed to say, 'The hotel across the way. I own it.'

'Then I am very sorry for you,' she said. As she lowered her gun, she saw something move in the bushes.

'Regard!' she shouted and pushed him clear as a soldier in armour came running at her, sword raised.

She pivoted round on the metal crutch and kicked him in the chest with her good leg. He reeled backwards and she swung the crutch, clubbing him neatly around the head.

He collapsed and lay still.

Pat was totally bewildered. 'Is it dead?' he said.

She leant against him, breathing heavily and searching the copse around them for further trouble. 'I can't tell. Come on, we're too exposed out here.'

'The hotel. You'd better come with me.'

Mordred had marched his men down the path beside the stone tower. Along the road ahead was a form of monument: a carven stone cross raised on a plinth. There were inscriptions on a bronze plate worked into the granite base.

Morgaine waited impatiently while her son studied the runes. When he turned to her, she recognized the frightened look he reserved for her impending anger.

'It is a shrine, to those fallen in battle,' he said.

'So they are not the savages you led us to believe,' she accused. 'You fought on their soil without proper respect for the dead.'

'Mother . . .'

Those brown eyes of his imploring her again. So like his father in every mannerism. The memories froze in her gullet.

'You have dishonoured us, Mordred. What is victory without honour? Leave us!'

He saluted coldly, turned and walked away along the road. She watched him go. He would return when his sulking was done.

In the meantime, the spirits of those knights they had dishonoured must be appeased. She formed the men-at-arms up before the shrine. They raised their swords in a grim salute to the dead.

As they stood in silent contemplation, she heard someone approaching on the road. She descended the steps to the lych gate and saw the figure of a man walking towards her. He seemed startled as she stepped out into his path.

'What manner of man are you?' she challenged.

Lethbridge-Stewart assumed the classic duelling position: the body turned sideways, the pistol held straight-armed and aimed at Morgaine.

The men-at-arms raised their weapons in threat. The Brigadier did not flinch.

Morgaine was impressed and greatly amused. 'A warrior, no less.' She faced his gun and enquired merrily, 'How goes the day?'

'I've had better,' said the Brigadier carefully.

'I am Morgaine Sunkiller,' she proclaimed imperiously. 'Dominator of the thirteen worlds and Battle Queen of the S'rax. What say you, sir warrior?'

He recognized the laws of parley and slowly lowered his pistol. 'I am Brigadier Lethbridge-Stewart. Surrender now and we can avoid bloodshed.'

She laughed. 'Are all your knights so resolute?'

'Bloody, bold and resolute, madam.'

'It is well.' She indicated the war memorial. 'No blood shall be spilled until we have done full honour to those of your warriors who have died in battle.'

'Let me see if I understand you correctly,' he said. 'You are holding a remembrance ceremony for the dead of our World Wars. A ceasefire to remain in force for the duration of said ceremony. Right?'

She nodded slowly. 'Your words are strange, but that is the meaning, yes.' She signalled the men-at-arms to lower their weapons.

The Brigadier holstered his gun. 'Very well. What must I do?'

They stood silently, side by side, while the men-at-arms knelt in ranks before the memorial. The Battle Queen and the veteran soldier. United in respect for one another's warriors and the etiquette of war.

After minutes had passed, Morgaine lifted her head and said,

'I wish you to know that I bear you no malice.'

'I understand,' he said.

'But when we meet again, I shall kill you.'

She turned, the sunlight glancing on her armour and her flowing red hair. She led her soldiers away along the road towards the village.

He would have been proud to lead such a well-drilled company. Nor did he doubt that they were formidable fighters. He was honoured that the Battle Queen deemed him a worthy opponent. But whether she had leapt from out of the past or from some other world where the laws of chivalry held sway, he could not tell.

It was imperative that he find the Doctor quickly. He retraced his steps back to where he had left Lavel, but there was no sign of her.

On the road, he saw a small blue car turning into the drive of a country hotel. He quickened his pace and started to run.

Chapter 3

Ace didn't need to see to tell that the pitch-black tunnel was damp. The cold air was clammy with vapour and the sound of dripping had increased. Her shoes, which she hadn't changed since she left Iceworld, were letting in water. She clung tightly to the Doctor's hand as they slipped and slithered their way along.

'Ancelyn's ancestors must have built this tunnel,' he was saying.

She kept on talking because she didn't want to stop and think about what she was doing. 'Professor?'

'Hmm?'

'Where does Ancelyn come from?'

'Another dimension,' said his voice. 'Sideways in time at a rough guess. A different universe.'

'Oh. Not a local boy then ...' She gave a gasp and swore as the floor slid under her and she sat in a puddle.

'Ace!' shouted the Doctor. 'Where are you?'

'I'm here!' She could hear him groping for her hand.

'Where? Why is there never light when I need it!'

There was a buzz and the tunnel walls gleamed with a tracery of phosphorescent green.

'Hey, Cavern Club!' grinned Ace. She turned towards the Doctor and gave a yell of fear as she saw the monstrous fish-head that loomed over them, its scimitar teeth bared.

Shou Yuing parked her 2CV in front of the Gore Crow. Her morning had consisted of arguments with her parents for not having rung home the night before. In the end, she had walked out again and come back to find Ace and the Doctor. If they had left the hotel, she had agreed to follow them to the dig.

The army officer running up the drive towards her didn't look as if he should be running at all. Too old, like a General from the Old Guard of the People's Republican Government.

'I'm commandeering your car,' he said.

'Excuse me?' said Shou Yuing.

He held out a hand. 'Give me the keys.'

'What?'

'The keys!'

She was too astonished to argue.

'Thank you,' he said and climbed into the 2CV.

Shou Yuing ran around the car and got into the passenger seat. 'Just a second, this is my car!'

'And I'm on urgent business, young lady. I'll ensure you are completely reimbursed for petrol and inconvenience.' He jammed the gears into reverse and backed his way out.

She looked at his cap badge. 'You're with UNIT, right?'

'What do you know about that, miss ...erm?'

'Li Shou Yuing. I met Brigadier Bambera.'

'Oh, really.' He turned the car on to the main road.

'Yes,' she said. She thought he would be impressed, but he kept driving.

'How did you get past the roadblock?' he said.

'Easy. They hadn't closed off the back lanes.'

He smiled and nodded. 'This Brigadier Bambera. I don't suppose she mentioned someone called the Doctor?'

The stone eyes of the fish gargoyle returned the Doctor and Ace's gaze. Its grotesque demon head blocked the entire end of the tunnel. Nostrils flared in its painted snout, above a cavernous maw that teemed with steel teeth like swords. It was the medieval depiction of the gates of hell.

'Just a portal,' said the Doctor. 'Clearly designed to frighten superstitious people off.'

'It gives me the creeps,' complained Ace.

'It is a little overtheatrical.'

He started to feel round the edge of the mouth. 'No coded pattern,' he muttered.

'No hidden switch?' she said.

He shook his head. 'Much too complicated.'

'Then how are we going to get inside?'

He turned, smiled knowingly and tapped the side of his nose. Then he straightened up, cleared his throat as if he was about to begin a recital, and said, 'It's me. Open up!'

With a grating clash, the steel teeth separated and slid up and downwards into the fish's jaws.

'I refuse to ask how you did that,' she said, staring into the dark throat beyond. 'How did you do that?'

He looked rather self-satisfied. 'It occurred to me that this tunnel was built to Merlin's designs.'

'But everyone thinks you're Merlin.'

'Exactly. The portal's keyed to my voice pattern. Just the sort of thing I'd do.' He stepped through the jaws into the darkness.

'Are you Merlin?' she called.

He reappeared and said, 'No,' and then added mysteriously, 'But I could be, in the future. My personal future, that is. Which could be the past.'

He vanished again.

Ace stood for a moment, grabbing at the loose ends he always left dangling for her to pick up. 'Right,' she said doubtfully and clambered through after him.

The darkness she had seen through the gate was a deep ocean half-light: green and cool. The place hummed gently and rythmically like something asleep.

The Doctor was silhouetted against a softer watery glow from the far end of a passage. He was running his hand across the glistening walls. The ribbed contours were solid and covered in organic patterns. Patches of light emanated at random along the walls and floor like the glow of deep-sea fish.

'Is this a submarine?' she said as she reached him. 'Or a spaceship?'

'More than that, this is a craft for travelling between dimensions.'

'It's more like being inside some huge animal,' she said.

He nodded and poked the wall with the tip of his umbrella. It quivered slightly and gurgled.

Ace stepped back in alarm. 'Who built it?'

'It wasn't built, it was grown.'

'Who grows spaceships?'

'Very advanced bioengineers.' He started to walk towards the light.

She had to walk sideways to ask questions and keep up with him. 'If it's grown, how does it fly then?'

'Magic!'

'Oh, what! Be feasible, Doctor.'

'I thought I was a Professor. What's Clarke's Law?'

They had reached an iris-shaped portal through which the light was filtered. She wondered why he always picked the most idiotic places to give her a science test. Since there was plainly no chance of going through until she had answered the question, she said in a singsong voice, 'Any sufficiently advanced technology is indistinguishable from magic.'

'Well, the reverse is also true.' He glanced at the portal and said, 'Come on, then!'

The grey sinews of the iris contracted. A circular hole opened through which light came in a mote-filled wave of greeting. He stepped through, and as Ace followed, she could not help saying aloud: 'Any sufficiently advanced form of magic is indistinguishable ... from technology.'

'Impressive,' said the Doctor. 'I knew you'd like it.'

The glare faded, leaving a single central beam of light descending from the high roof. It lit a great sword which stood upright, its blade embedded in a block of obsidian. Its hilt was ornamented with a single pommel amethyst.

Beyond the sword, half in shadow, was a raised plinth on which a knight in black armour lay, still as a statue. His mail-gloved hands were laid on his breast in an attitude of prayer.

The Doctor and Ace slowly approached the pool of light. Little eddies of centuries-old dust swirled up from the floor as they passed. Their footsteps echoed high into the rib-vaulted roof.

'That's Arthur, King of the Britons, isn't it?' whispered Ace.

The Doctor stopped and laid a hand on her arm. His voice, so often mocking, was full with a quiet awe. 'This is the legendary King Arthur. From another dimension, where the man is closer to the myth.' He frowned. 'I wonder what he's doing here.'

'Not a lot,' said Ace.

As he suspected, the filigree inlay on the sword's blade was reminiscent of circuitry in the TARDIS. This was what had summoned him. 'The King's in suspended animation,' he said.

Ace placed one hand on the sword hilt and threw out the other in mock declamation. 'In eternal sleep until the hour of England's greatest need!'

'Ace, leave that alone!' scolded the Doctor.

She planted her other hand on the hilt as well. 'Don't worry, Professor. I've seen *The Sword in the Stone*. It's not like I'm the King of England.'

She gave a playful tug at the sword.

'Ace, no!'

The sword slid, almost sprang, out of the stone.

'Gordon Bennett!' She fell backwards under the weapon's weight, throwing up a whole cumulus of dust.

The Doctor began to help her up, his eyes darting around the vast shadowy chamber. 'I hope you didn't disturb anything,' he snapped.

'It disturbed me,' complained Ace as she dusted herself down.

'I hope you didn't disturb anything else!' He could already hear a low keening in the darkness.

He searched around again. If he was Merlin, what sort of defences would he put into such a ship? And where would he put its fail-safe systems? It was bound not to be a straight-forward job. His predilection to be too clever for his own good had earned him a certain notoriety amongst his companions. So many regenerations in so short a span could not be good for the brain.

And why had Merlin forgotten, as he designed the wretched thing, that one day in the future he had been its victim? Bother! There was too much here that he did not like. He hated temporal paradoxes and he particularly disliked working with organic technology: a nasty, messy business.

89

Who said that he had to be Merlin anyway? There was an infinite number of possibilities. But it seemed that the more he struggled, the more tangled he became in the web of the very thing that he always denied.

He caught a flicker of green light at the edge of his vision. That thing was already stalking him in the darkness and whatever trick he tried, he doubted he would escape it.

What had Ancelyn said so merrily? That he knew Merlin by his manner, not his aspect? And Mordred recognized him too, though plainly not by his current face. Between them, they had as good as passed his death sentence.

The threat often hung over him, frequently inspiring him. But when its event was thus predicted, it came like a hammer blow. That he would regenerate was certain, for the evidence of his inescapable future as Merlin was all around him. But before that was achieved, he knew as surely as he now lived, that he was going to die ... again.

'Doctor,' shouted Ace and pointed into the shadows.

A ribbon-tail of green light slithered behind one of the consoles that surrounded the chamber like pews.

Whatever it was, whatever it resembled, it was the manifestation of his destiny. The more he resisted the future, the closer it slid.

He reached for her hand. 'Ace, I think it's time for Plan B.'

'We run?'

A venomous green head reared up over the console. Its snakemouth gaped open in a hiss of malice.

'Yes!' he shouted.

They began to run towards the portal, but the snake launched itself into the air, wriggling through the darkness like an ethereal tapeworm.

It blocked their path.

'What do we do?' shouted Ace, lifting the sword towards the attacker.

'Now is not the time to panic!'

The ghost snake was casting its head about until its white eyes set upon a target. It homed on the Doctor and struck at his face. He caught a blast of blue light on his upheld arm and went skidding across the floor.

'Now we can panic,' he gasped as Ace started to pull him up.

The snake was slowly circling in the air like a shark sizing up its victims.

'It's a form of automated defence system, isn't it?' said Ace.

'Yes.' He saw the snake turn towards them. 'When I say run, run . . .'

The snake bore down on him like a glowing javelin.

'Run!' he yelled, and they split up as the snake coursed through the gap.

The Doctor saw Ace, still carrying the sword and running towards an alcove in the wall. He tried to call her back, but the snake struck at him again as it passed over his head. His hat tumbled, smoking, to the floor.

'Not that way!' he shouted at Ace.

She turned inside the alcove and called, 'It's a dead end.'

The recess suddenly filled with white light. A glass door slammed down over the entrance.

The snake had begun to circle again, as if the defence system had been curtailed during this diversion.

The Doctor reached the door in two seconds flat. Ace was beating her hands against the glass, but he could not hear her.

'Hang on. I'll soon have you out,' he mouthed at her.

Ace took no notice. She was lifting her feet awkwardly and pointing down. Water was splashing around her ankles and up the glass. There were jets hosing down the back of the alcove from above. She was trapped in the ship's airlock.

She started to beat against the glass again as he searched for the controls to the door. The grey and chilling lake water was already up to her waist and rising fast.

He could find nothing. He saw her starting to tread water as the torrent reached her shoulders.

'Let go of the sword!' he shouted.

He saw her suddenly trying to point behind him. Looking up, he saw the ghost snake rushing in. Its blast caught him squarely on the chest, sending him hurtling across the floor to collide head on with one of the consoles.

Ace struggled and went under for the first time.

Part 3

Scenario: Bent Spear

'...*and in the midst of the lake Arthur was ware
of an arm clothed in white samite, that held
a fair sword in that hand.*'

Sir Thomas Malory
Le Morte D'Arthur

Chapter 1

A cold wind was whipping up waves on Vortigern's Lake. Bambera and Ancelyn emerged from the woods along the shoreline between the dig and the UNIT convoy.

A figure stood on a bare outcrop that jutted into the water. His anorak was drawn tightly around him as he stared unmoving across the lake.

Soldiers came running to meet Bambera. Ancelyn kept his distance while she stood in conference with them, but he watched as more soldiers came from the huddle of ugly machines by the water. They held her in high honour, standing formally around her, while she issued orders and listened to their intelligence. It occurred to Ancelyn that in this place, Brigadier might be a nobler title for a warrior than that of Knight General in the world.

Bambera pointed at the machines and then at the crater that lay along the bank surrounded by an area of freshly flung mud. The soldiers pointed at the solitary figure on the outcrop. They all turned and stared at Ancelyn.

He bowed his head in acknowledgement. His wrists still bore red wheals from the handcuffs in which he had allowed her to imprison him.

Bambera yelled his name and started to walk towards the lone figure. The knight followed his lady.

'Doctor Warmsly?' called Bambera as they reached the water's edge.

He did not move, but they heard him say, 'You've probably never thought about it, but it takes one year to uncover one centimetre on a site this big . . .'

His voice had a dry quaver that was only just under control. He took a step towards the water.

'What are you doing?' said Bambera.

He would not turn and look at them. 'I came to get away from the wreck that girl made of my work.'

She touched his shoulder. 'Are you OK?'

'I just need some peace and quiet.'

Since childhood Warmsly had heard the distant horns of Arthur's world calling. He loved Tennyson and T.H. White, and he knew Malory by heart. The site by the lake was his discovery and it had been his slow painstaking love to uncover the history of his dig. No help, no grants from the cold, commercial world.

The history and the romance of Arthur were separate realities and he loved them both. One for the head and one for the heart. But he knew in which world he truly belonged.

'Why do you dig holes in the ground?' said the yellow-haired man who dressed like a pageant knight.

'To uncover the past,' said Peter gloomily.

'Do you not have songs for that?'

'Songs?'

'You know,' said Bambera, 'an oral history.'

Peter rounded on them accusingly. 'Oh yes, we have songs, stories, poems. The trouble is they get it wrong, don't they. They distort history. I'm looking for the truth.'

'Such as?' said Bambera.

'King Arthur,' he replied.

Ancelyn lifted his head and stared into the cold wind. 'The High King.'

Peter shook his head. 'This site is one of the places where they say the final battle between Arthur and Mordred was fought. And this lake is where Bedivere threw Excalibur.' He ignored Ancelyn's eager gaze and turned back to the empty water. 'It's all rubbish, of course!'

It was a few seconds before the Doctor could drag himself back into consciousness.

Not dead yet.

He struggled to his feet and tried to reach the alcove.

Ace was still there, kicking in the churning water. Fighting to keep her head above the rising surface.

Overhead, high in the chamber, the snake circled. Waiting to swoop again.

Still he could find no way of reaching her. 'Why isn't there a central control?' he shouted in desperation.

Instantly, a small cavity squelched open in a wall across the chamber. He reached eagerly for the hole, but caught sight of a green glow brightening on the wall.

He ducked and the ghost snake barrelled over his head.

The swirling water had filled the alcove, but he saw the kick of Ace's legs and the glint of the sword.

At the cavity's heart, there was a pallid nodule the size of a fist. The ship's organic core. Blue-shelled digits like the legs of a lobster agitated against its pulsing surface. The Doctor grasped the nodule and wrenched it from its place. It dripped white gel as it continued pulsing rhythmically in his hand. Ganglia strands trailed back into the ruptured cavity.

He ignored the snake as it wriggled slowly nearer. Holding the nodule in both hands, he concentrated his thoughts and squeezed.

The cavity gave a shrill squeal and the digits scrabbled at nothing. In an explosion of giant bubbles, the water in the alcove vanished upwards, sucked away by pressure as a hatch opened in its roof.

Ace vanished with it.

The Doctor stood back, unsure whether to be relieved or worried.

The snake hovered a foot from his head, its tail moving behind it in slithy undulation.

He tried to avoid its malignant eyes. Tried to convince himself that he would never design a device that was a killer. It couldn't hurt him. It was simply used to frighten off superstitious peasants.

No, no. Stop. He was starting to think of himself as Merlin. He must not fall into that trap.

He was held by the snake's predatory stare. 'Go away, little tapeworm,' he said casually.

The snake slipped nearer.

Hardly daring to move, the Doctor fingered the wet surface of the control core. But his hands could not reproduce the precision instrumentation needed to manipulate the organic device.

The snake's jaws opened, revealing fangs like curved needles. The emanation hissed and flicked its barbed tongue.

'No, you won't hurt me,' said the Doctor. 'You can't. Not unless someone else has tampered with you...'

He squeezed the core again. Gently.

A portal at the far end of the chamber widened and closed again.

That was wrong.

He teased another section of the core with his thumb.

The green of the snake deepened. Its eyes glittered with livid malice.

'If I don't live to be Merlin, you could be in trouble,' he added. 'Sorry, but I can't stand here all day.'

He jabbed a finger at the pulsing core.

The whole ship lurched. The back of the snake's head flared out like a cobra's hood and went on expanding in a green curve until it finally enveloped him.

He struggled as tingling coils of light plasma wound around him. With a spasm, he dropped the slippery core and fell backwards.

The snake tightened its grip.

On the floor, the core throbbed in a pool of gel. Its ganglia twitched and curled helplessly just out of the Doctor's flailing reach.

Shou Yuing sat in the passenger seat of her car and prayed. The Brigadier was a good driver, but he was taking the corners too fast. Her 2CV was H reg: one of the last made. Her brother had only given it a respray last week.

'Please be careful,' she said and clung to her seat belt. She could already hear new rattles that she hadn't heard before.

'And the Doctor said something about examining the dig?'

said the Brigadier brusquely.

'Yes. He kept on about finding new evidence.'

When they reached the hill overlooking the lake, she saw Ace's new crater where the site should have been.

'What's going on? Someone's bombed out the dig!'

The Brigadier smiled.

He brought the car to an abrupt stop beside Peter Warmsly's Range Rover and got out. Shou Yuing clambered out of her side and yelled after him. He still had her car keys.

'Stay clear,' he called back and drew his gun.

He ignored the three figures standing on the headland and the cluster of military vehicles stationed further along the bank. Instead, he headed towards the crater and soon vanished into its depths.

'What do you know of Excalibur?' said Ancelyn to Doctor Warmsly. He glanced quickly at Bambera, who shrugged vaguely and stared out at the lake.

Peter shivered. 'King Arthur's sword Excalibur, wrought by the lonely maiden of the lake,' he said. 'She rose up out of the water, holding the sword Excalibur aloft.'

'This lake?' asked Ancelyn eagerly.

A warmth returned to Peter's disheartened voice. ' "Thou rememberest how, in those old days, one summer noon, an arm rose up from out the bosom of the lake, clothed in white samite, mystic and wonderful, holding the sword. And how I rode across and took it, and have worn it like a king." '

How strange it seemed to the knight, to hear the people of Avallion retell the story of his own ancestors. The drab words of their speech caught fire when they recalled the moments of their history touched by that of the real world.

'I told you it's just a myth,' added Peter. 'Honestly, women in water, holding swords.' He shook his head in gloom.

'Look!' yelled Bambera. She pointed out at the lake.

Something flashed on the water twenty metres out. A sword was rising above the grey-green waves. It was held by an arm dressed in shiny black material. A head broke the surface and flung itself back, gasping for air.

'It's that blasted girl,' shouted Peter and he began to wade out into the waves.

When the water surged upwards out of the airlock alcove, Ace had felt the sword wrench her arm up above her head.

It seemed to cut a path through the water as bubbles seethed in a rising column and carried her with them. She was aware of a sudden vast darkness around her, and of a green crustacean hull that sank away below.

Excalibur lifted her towards a flat sky surface of grey ripples where existence seemed to end. After the cold water, there was a shock of cold air as she burst into the world. It was that which took the breath she had held away.

The sword was still light in her hand, so light that she was sure she could use it as a float if she needed it. After moments of treading water, she heard shouts in the distance. She saw figures on the shore and struck out towards them.

The world vanished. The ghost snake's coils wrapped over the Doctor's head and shut out air and reality. His one free hand stretched blindly for the pulsing core of the ship and found only dust. The fingers flailed in a desperate attempt to snatch at anything.

The Doctor's chest tightened under the crush. He was suffocating. The envelope of green light slid around him, reducing his awareness to imagination. His normal defence of self-induced coma was out of reach. His thoughts reeled uncontrolled. His future lives began to flash before him.

Merlin again.

Too late for that now. Someone else's problem. Not his. Morgaine could find an adversary elsewhere. Even if he had lived, he would never be, nor ever have been, Merlin.

Ectoplasm choked him.

Somewhere in his memory, a voice was lecturing: 'There is a degree of injury beyond which any bodily regeneration is impossible for a Time Lord.'

The aged Prydonian science tutor had scoured the class for the pupil who was paying least attention.

'And that point is? You!'

The young student went pale. 'Total death,' he intoned.

It was the first time that the possibility of a final inescapable doom had occurred to him.

Total death in livid green squirmed around the Doctor. But darkness fringed with blood red crept in from the sides.

Merlin! This is all your fault!

A big solid army boot squelched down on the core. The ganglia twisted in a spasm of shock. Gel spewed across the floor.

Across the hall, the strangling coils of the ghost snake exploded in shards of light and evaporated.

The Doctor sat up and gasped in the dank air. He was shaking. He looked up at the uniformed figure who approached and crouched before him.

'I just can't let you out of my sight, can I Doctor?'

The Doctor's face split with a broad grin. 'Brigadier Alastair Gordon Lethbridge-Stewart. So you recognized me then.'

'Yes. Who else would it be?' said the Brigadier. He looked down at his boot and grimaced. 'Excuse me, Doctor, I seem to have trodden in something nasty.'

The Doctor got to his feet and began to dust himself down. 'I think we all have, Brigadier. Right up to our necks.'

Ace waded out of the lake with the sword and faced the three figures on the bank. 'Surf's up,' she said bitterly.

Peter Warmsly, his head shaking slowly, stared at her in disbelief.

'What are you doing in the lake?' said Bambera.

'Drowning,' snapped Ace and handed the sword to Ancelyn. 'Here, you can be King of England,' she said.

Shou Yuing dashed up and skidded to a halt. 'What have I missed?' she gasped.

Ancelyn turned the blade of the sword so that its runes caught the light. ' 'Tis Excalibur,' he said in awe.

Ace shivered. 'That's what I said, Shakespeare.'

'Damosel, where did you find this?'

'And where's the Doctor?' butted in Bambera.

'In a spaceship under the lake.' Ace said it casually to shock them. 'He's in trouble. I have to help him.'

She pushed through them and started to head for the crater. Somewhere she had left her bag with another can of nitro.

She heard Bambera's voice behind her. 'Come back here, you!'

'Piss off!' she retaliated and kept walking.

Bambera caught her by the arm. 'You listen to me, young lady. I'm in charge here until this emergency is over.'

'Not for long, you're not,' said Shou Yuing as she raced up behind.

'What?'

The Chinese girl winced. 'There's a Brigadier Lethbridge-Stewart here, looking for you.'

Bambera's eyes widened. 'Lethbridge-Stewart? Where? How do you know?'

'We came from the village in my car. He went to look at that hole.'

To Ace's astonishment, Bambera began to run towards the crater. Shou Yuing began to giggle, but then she saw that Ace's face was like a thundercloud.

They caught up with Bambera as she stood on the rim of the crater. The pit below was empty.

'Down there?' she said.

Shou Yuing shrugged. 'Yes.'

Ace pointed to the half-buried tunnel entrance. 'He's in there. The Doctor said it was a trap. It lets you in, but it doesn't let you out.'

She and Shou Yuing started down the slope, but Bambera grabbed and pulled them back up. To her annoyance, she saw Dr Warmsly and Ancelyn approaching.

'What uniform was Lethbridge-Stewart wearing?' she said and touched her UNIT cap badge. 'Did he have an insignia like this?'

'A bit,' said Shou Yuing. She looked down into the crater again and pointed. 'But more like that!'

Ace breathed a sigh of relief. Two figures were struggling out of the tunnel. The Doctor, covered in dust, his hat charred, was deep in conversation with an elderly man who Ace didn't know. He was a solid, no-nonsense army type in fatigues and a peaked cap.

'Why hasn't King Arthur woken up yet?' he said.

'I don't know,' said the Doctor. 'Perhaps it's just a matter of time.'

The man smiled at the Doctor like an old friend and said, 'Perhaps he's just a late riser.' He pointed to the welcoming committee ranged above them along the crater edge.

'Professor,' shouted Ace.

'Ace! Thank goodness.'

Bambera saluted. 'Brigadier Lethbridge-Stewart.' She negotiated the slope with as much dignity as she could muster. 'I thought you'd retired,' she said cheerfully.

'So did I, Brigadier Bambera.' He returned her salute. 'Now, is the exclusion perimeter secure? The whole area is crawling with armed extra-terrestrials and they're hostile!'

Ace watched the Doctor indulge himself in a sly smile. 'Just like old times, eh Brigadier?' he said.

She waited to be introduced.

Bambera looked awkward. 'Regrettably I've only just got back here myself. But my first officer informs me that the radio jamming suddenly stopped a few minutes ago.'

She found Lethbridge-Stewart manoeuvring her to one side. 'The Doctor said there'd been problems. So we'd better get started, hadn't we?'

'That's right,' interrupted the Doctor with a grin. 'Two brigadiers are better than one!'

As he started up the slope towards Ace, she heard him mutter, 'I hope.'

'Ace, you're sopping wet,' he said out loud.

'My lord Merlin?' called Ancelyn.

The Doctor veered off course, leaving Ace alone and disgruntled.

Lethbridge-Stewart turned in surprise. 'Merlin now?' he asked.

'He has many names,' said the knight. 'Soon we shall see the tyrant Morgaine bow before his power.'

He went down on one knee and lifted Excalibur towards the

102

Doctor. Lowering his eyes, he said, 'Truly, the Time of Restitution has come.'

What about me, thought Ace. I brought that back.

The Doctor seemed almost reluctant to take the sacred weapon. He picked it out of Ancelyn's hands and handed it to Peter Warmsly. 'Hold this, Peter. it goes with the scabbard. Look after it for me.'

The archaeologist was too confused even to answer.

The Brigadier climbed the crater and studied the group. 'He has many companions too,' he said and nodded at Ace. 'This must be the latest one.'

Ace stared.

'I'll get the perimeter checked now,' said Bambera and turned to go.

'Bambera,' called Lethbridge-Stewart. 'I had to leave my helicopter pilot where we came down near the village. Lieutenant Lavel. She may be hurt and in trouble. We may have to get her out of there.'

'I'll see what I can do.'

'And see if you can find a blanket for this young lady,' he added with a glance at Ace.

Bambera looked at him and said tightly, 'Yes, sir. Perhaps I should make some tea too.' She walked stiffly away towards the group of soldiers staring from the convoy barrier tape.

They heard her yelling orders. Ancelyn bowed his head to Merlin and set off in her wake.

Ace found that Lethbridge-Stewart was watching her. 'Are you all right, miss?' he enquired.

'Just call me the Latest One,' she said sourly and started to walk after Bambera. 'I'll get my own blanket. Coming, Shou Yuing?'

The Brigadier found himself alone with the Doctor and the archaeologist. 'Oh dear. Women. Not really my field,' he said. And he had forgotten to ring Doris as well.

The Doctor flicked away a charred piece of his hat. He thought of Morgaine and studied the woods that surrounded the lake. 'Don't worry Brigadier, people will be shooting at you soon,' he said cheerfully.

Chapter 2

Elizabeth Rowlinson sat quietly and listened. It was ten minutes since she and Pat had heard the helicopter come down beyond the trees.

The phone was still out of order and none of the staff had turned up that morning, but there were no new customers either. The hotel had seemed mercifully empty once the visitors had vanished. When they heard the crash, Pat had taken the first-aid kit and gone to help.

Elizabeth waited in the lounge bar and strained to hear the familiar sounds that no one else noticed. She had felt presences too. Since the strange night before, instincts that she kept to herself warned her that the world had somehow changed or was out of kilter. She had even sensed what she supposed was darkness. The change was beyond her definition, but it was unnatural and filled her with fear.

She moved to the window where she could feel the sunlight. The more she strained to hear, the less she heard. The silence nearly deafened her. She could no longer tell what she listened for from what she imagined she heard.

She thought she heard many footsteps on the road, marching in unison like soldiers. The sun's warmth faded as she felt a shadow pass across the window.

She thought she heard the outer door to the hall open. She even felt the brief chill of a sudden draught. Then there was silence; a silence that was too full of quiet.

She fumbled for her white stick and started to tap her way across the floor. Twice she collided with chairs that were not in their normal places.

She had almost reached the door when her stick tapped metal. She paused, sensing a presence and hearing breathing. There was a smell of man's sweat.

'Pat?' she said and put out a hand to find a shoulder.

Her fingers touched cold metal that curved around its wearer's shape.

Elizabeth snatched away her hand and tried to back off. 'Who are you? What do you want?' she said.

The presence did not move.

No one answered.

'Pat, come quickly. Patrick!'

A cold hand gloved in fine chain mail seized her wrist.

'Pat!' she screamed.

Excalibur's cry had ceased. Morgaine's power was not so diminished that she could not hear the sword's sudden silence.

The Knight Commander of the Queen's entourage awaited orders. One hundred men-at-arms, summoned at Morgaine's behest through the rent between worlds, stood in ranks in a marshy field. One hundred red cloaks shifted in the wind.

Tempered steel among tufts of meadow flowers.

She had broken the bridge across the abyss behind her soldiers and healed the wound in time with her arts. Her quest was irrevocable. They would not see the world again until her needs were fulfilled.

Those natives of Avallion they had encountered since leaving the shrine had scuttled away in fear before them. They had been rough peasant stock, not the warrior nobility that the Knight Brigadier had represented.

The summons of the King's sword had been for her; and so she had answered and the calling had ceased. Yet was it also for her to choose the meeting place? Or was this yet another of Merlin's tricks? For surely Arthur was oath-bound never to step beyond the rules of chivalry?

Yet there had been one time, one moment, when all gallantry had failed the High King. And that moment of dishonour burned daily in her heart.

So be it. Let Merlin play his games of Blind Mole's Bluff, she would make her first move now and trounce him at every turn. The sword, symbol of power, would be hers.

'Knight Commander,' she said. 'The final confrontation is at hand. Where is my son?'

'At the hostelry, my lady,' said the young voice.

She stared at the reflection of herself in his mirrored umberere visor. She had wanted a son with a dedication to his duties as a prince, not a wayward who used his rank to behave like a noble ruffian. Time and again for a thousand years, Mordred's indiscretions and immodesties caused embarrassment to the royal household; and always they seemed unerringly aimed at her.

She bestowed upon her son every exaltation that his position merited, but there were always a hundred young knights who were more worthy of all his honours and who showed their queen more dedication.

For all her powers, Morgaine could not choose her child. But she would unleash those powers on any other who stood in her path.

'Bid the men be ready,' she said. 'Merlin has possession of Excalibur and must be dealt with.'

'My lady.'

She pointed to the hard track that led into the trees. 'Take your men along the road yonder. Seek out those that hold Excalibur and take the sword from them.'

'And if they resist us?' he said.

She knew what he feared, for she had faced Merlin long, long ago. Merlin's deeds were ancient tales to this young knight, but she had seen the dragon that he summoned to Breceliande to melt the ice in which she bound him. The songs that were sung of his power over light, darkness and the elementals were all founded in truth.

She, Morgaine, the Rose of Hell, feared none of that infernal region's horrors and infections as much as she dreaded one glance of Merlin's mocking eyes.

But she must have Excalibur; no matter the cost.

'If they resist you, give them an honourable death.'

By the time the Brigadiers had finished a round of briefings with Major Husak of the Czech engineering group and Lieutenant Richards, the Doctor was on his fourth cup of army tea.

When they emerged from the sealed end of the Command Vehicle after talks with Geneva, the Doctor had reached his fifth cup. Bambera seemed in an altogether better humour and Lethbridge-Stewart was wearing a satisfied smile which could only mean he was up to something.

Or worse, that there would be fighting soon.

The Doctor had packed Ace and Shou Yuing out of the way of any talk of combat. Although he suspected they would be saying something very unladylike to a couple of squaddies who had been eyeing them up.

He had spent a profitable time getting Ancelyn to talk to Peter Warmsly. The archaeologist seemed to be responding well to the knight's tales, but the Doctor was unsure how deeply the man was still in shock.

Sitting tightly in a deep leather seat, Peter clung to Excalibur and said, 'I keep thinking you're true, young man. I think I'd like that. It's better than reality, isn't it?'

And there were tears welling in his eyes.

The Doctor pocketed a small notebook into which he had scribbled a few notes from Ancelyn's stories. Just a few references to another universe that paralleled the one he knew; nothing to do with Merlin or an inescapable future that was getting a little too close for comfort. But better safe than sorry for all that.

'Well?' he said to either of the Brigadiers.

'We have full clearance for whatever action we need to take,' said Bambera.

'Within the exclusion zone,' added Lethbridge-Stewart. 'Under UN resolution . . .'

'Oh, never mind all that,' snapped the Doctor. 'As long as you're not going to meet Morgaine's forces head on.' He noticed the two soldiers give each other the briefest of glances.

'Good Lord, no,' the Brigadier reassured him. 'Not without knowing their strengths.'

'I'm delighted to hear it,' said the Doctor. He helped himself to sugar, but found he had already finished the tea without it.

'Strengths are something that you can tell us about, Ancelyn,' said Bambera.

The Knight looked startled. 'My lady Winifred?'

Bambera's voice tone stayed urgent, but the manner cooled a little. 'We need to know Morgaine's resources. How many men she has, their weaponry.'

'Purely for our own defence,' said Lethbridge-Stewart.

Ancelyn's noble face assumed an expression of deepest concern. 'My lady, is this honourable? Must I betray the very men I have served with?'

'Excuse me, gentlemen,' said Bambera. She took Ancelyn's arm and drew him as far aside as the Command Vehicle would allow, which was hardly aside at all. Everyone heard.

'What are you playing at, Ancelyn? You're not a one-man army. And we're not playing knights in armour.'

'Then hear me out, lady,'

'Call me "my lady" again and I'll break your nose!'

Ancelyn turned from her, smiled bravely and addressed the group as one. 'I came to Avallion, your world, to answer Merlin's summons. If you are his followers then I shall add my strength to yours, but I cannot betray my brothers-in-arms.'

'You seem prepared to fight them,' said Lethbridge-Stewart.

'Aye. With all my heart.'

'Then why won't you tell us?' exploded Bambera. 'It's all right to use the information for yourself, is it?' Her irritation was already well stoked, but she turned and found a new coal to add to the fire: the Doctor was staring intently into his empty cup and smiling to himself.

To her astonishment, and perhaps his, the next voice to speak belonged to Dr Peter Warmsly.

'For Ancelyn, the fight is honourable. To betray even an old ally would be unthinkable. His whole training as a knight is embodied in that code. It's all formal etiquette, you see. Glorious stuff.'

'Thank you, Peter,' said the Doctor quietly.

'The Doctor speaks the truth,' said Ancelyn. 'And Merlin understands also.'

'Ah,' said the Doctor. 'That's something we should have a little chat about.'

But Ancelyn was already brimming with optimism. 'Be assured my friends, Merlin and Arthur will lead us to victory. For I can tell you that Morgaine's power of magic wanes like the moon in this place. This is alien ground for her. It was always so away from the world.'

'So she won't attack,' said Bambera. 'She'll be cautious.'

'She seemed fairly belligerent when I came across her,' said Lethbridge-Stewart.

'That was always her way,' agreed Ancelyn. 'But caution is her watchword. She will not raise arms until she knows how it lies with her enemy and their weaknesses. She talks of honour, but her true way is treachery.'

'Good,' said Lethbridge-Stewart. 'Then it won't take many men to deal with her. Now what I suggest, Bambera, is this . . .'

'Brigadiers . . . both of you!' The Doctor was tapping his fingers against his knee in annoyance. His little chats always seemed to turn into full-blown war councils. 'Morgaine is a powerful adept in occult science and sorcery. She may even have power above that of an Ipsissimus.'

Ancelyn grinned again. 'Only you, Merlin, match her in the strategy of magic.'

'Really, Doctor?' said Lethbridge-Stewart. 'I thought you once told me there was no such thing.'

The Doctor looked flustered. 'Yes, yes. That's as may be. There's magic and there's "magic". And before you ask, Brigadier, an Ipissimus is the highest grade in power a magician, a human magician, has ever attained . . . so far. It makes any Magisters you may have come across look like hocus-pocus fairground performers.'

'Thank you, Doctor,' said Lethbridge-Stewart wearily.

'You're not up against a rabble of medieval vassals,' the Doctor went on. 'Morgaine's people have the technology to jump between universes amd grow living spaceships. More than that, I guess she can summon up powers you can't defeat with a bazooka.'

Ancelyn nudged Bambera and whispered gleefully, 'He knows all this already. It's his way to tease.'

For a moment, Bambera smiled. She looked at the Doctor with growing respect. 'But there's no way she can know our forces or strategy.'

'Oh yes, my lady,' said Ancelyn. 'She has her ways to make a tongue prattle.'

'But how will she know?' mocked Bambera. 'What does she have? A surveillance network of medieval satellites? All my men are accounted for. No one's going to talk.'

Lethbridge-Stewart gave a sudden heavy sigh. As the others turned to look at him, he said quietly, 'Lavel.'

Chapter 3

The column of men-at-arms had taken two full minutes to pass along the road.

As their marching faded, Pat Rowlinson raised his head above the level of the hedge. He saw the column making a right wheel into the road that led towards Vortigern's Lake.

'What is this?' asked Françoise Lavel. 'The village where time stood still?'

'I don't know,' said Pat. 'I don't know what's happening. I thought you'd tell me that. Who are those people?'

Lavel shrugged. 'I don't know either. That's the trouble with UNIT. The work's so security-bound, sometimes even we don't know what we're working on.'

'Or can't tell a civilian,' he said knowingly. 'I was in the police force twenty-three years. I know what it's like.'

She winced with the pain of her leg.

'We'd better get inside,' said Pat. 'I don't like it out here. After last night, it's too quiet. I haven't seen a car this morning.'

'That'll be the *zone sanitaire*,' she said. 'The exclusion zone. Has nobody told you?'

'Nobody's told us anything.' He helped her along a path beside the hedgerow until they reached a freshly kreosoted fence. There was a gap halfway along, where it had been brought down by the storm.

'How much further?' she asked. She tried not to lean her

weight on him, but her leg was painful.

'Just through here and up to the hotel.' As he started to help
her through the gap, she stared back at the woods, looking for
danger.

'Come on,' he insisted. 'I left my wife on her own.'

'You go ahead. I think I can walk.'

'I won't ask if you can look after yourself,' he said with a
glance at her gun. 'I'll check the coast is clear.'

He made his way through the garden up to the hotel. For a
moment he paused as he found the back door wide open.

There was a stranger in the house. He wore a full suit of
armour and a heavy sword at his belt. His hair was long, dark
and unkempt. He leant against the bar amidst the empty pint
glasses and stared at Pat with a sneer. Elizabeth, who was pulling
yet another pint, turned her head as she heard someone enter.

'Pat? Is that you?' Her voice was choked with terror.

'Elizabeth.' He pushed behind the bar and embraced her
tightly. She was shaking. 'It's all right, I'm here now,' he
whispered gently.

He looked at the saturnine stranger, who leered drunkenly
back across the bar at them.

'Your wife?' said Mordred.

'Yes.'

The Prince raised his glass to them. 'With your aspect, it is
well that she is blind.' He laughed and drained his beer messily.
It ran in trickles down his unshaven chin.

'Get out,' Pat wanted to say, but the words cloyed in his
throat.

'Speak up, landlord.' Mordred turned and sat in an armchair.
'Do you not want my custom?'

There were footsteps in the hall. Lavel walked unsteadily into
the lounge, her gun drawn. She saw Pat and said, 'Someone's
coming. There's a woman in armour . . .'

She noticed Mordred and froze.

'What is this?' said the Prince. His interest was suddenly
aroused by the intruder.

Lavel pushed back her hair and levelled the gun at him.

'So there is light in this grey world,' he said.

112

'Don't move.' She faced him awkwardly, trying to put her weight on her good leg.

'Am I to do nothing?' he teased. He stayed lounging in the chair, fixing her with his eyes, mocking her, daring her.

'*Vous pouvez payer l'addition*,' she said tightly. 'Pay the bill if you like.'

'Light and fire!' He lurched eagerly to his feet. 'Come drink with me.'

'I said don't move!'

She was frightened and that excited him.

'I could wish for kinder words,' he said and stepped closer.

Lavel tried to steady the gun, but the fierce concentration of his dark eyes burned and beguiled her.

He reached for her weapon hand.

'Mordred. Who is this?'

A woman's imperious voice cut through Lavel's struggling thoughts. The pilot backed away and turned to cover the new-comer with the gun.

Behind the bar, the Rowlinsons cowered, innocent bystanders in the power play of forgotten beings.

A tall woman in golden armour was watching Lavel. Her straight red-gold hair was like fine silk and reached to her waist.

A brief look of resigned contempt crossed Mordred's face. 'She's a warrior maid,' he said.

Morgaine stepped forward, keeping Lavel in the full glare of her scrutiny. 'A woman? Good. I would know the strength of their forces.'

She studied the gun that Lavel was aiming at her.

'I will shoot,' warned the terrified pilot.

The Queen smiled and placed her hand over the end of the muzzle.

Lavel saw that she could not escape. She began to weep as the trigger pulled at her finger.

The gun fired.

Morgaine opened her hand, letting metal dust trickle between her fingers.

Lavel tried to understand and failed. '*C'est impossible*,' she whispered and all her energy drained.

'Be silent,' said Morgaine quietly.

Lavel's mouth closed with a snap. Her gun clattered to the floor.

'Rest here and tell me,' crooned Morgaine.

The helpless woman sank to her knees and bowed her head in deference. Her temples were cradled in the hands of the Battle Queen, as a fretful child is soothed by its mother. Or a predator starts its feed.

Morgaine sighed as visions in her head clouded her sight. She closed her eyes.

Lavel started to scream.

'Hush, child. Gently, gently,' whispered Morgaine's voice, but it sounded an age away.

Lavel quietened and stopped trembling.

The stream of memories eased into a steady flow. A laughing child in the fields of a land called Brittany. Wide beaches of sand and distant fishing boats on the blue-grey sea. Françoise Eloise Lavel. *'Non, je m'appelle Çoisique!'*

Seabirds wheeled in the sunlight. *'Oh petite mère, je veux voler. Voler comme une grande flèche.'*

'Valkyrie 9 to Control. It's strange, but since I've been in UNIT I no longer think in French.'

'United Nations Intelligence Taskforce. It's worse than the Sorbonne with firearms! Top security *de rigeur* ...'

In moments, Morgaine understood the terms and resources of her enemies. The laughing child's thoughts were her thoughts. She inherited new memories of a past that was stolen. And with these were the joy and heartbreak of another's life.

Adieu, adieu, ma pauvre petite. Maintenant tu es avec moi.

She released the head, leaving Lavel kneeling in motionless catalepsy.

'Now we know, Mordred,' said the Queen, and she turned to leave.

Elizabeth Rowlinson tried to pull Pat back to safety as he rose warily from behind the bar. 'You can't just leave her like that,' he cried in a rage.

Morgaine stared at him. A peasant that dared raise its voice to her. 'You are right,' she said coldly.

114

She threw out her arm towards Lavel in a gesture of dismissal. There was a blaze of light in which the mindless body of Françoise Eloise disintegrated and dispersed to nothing. A choking smell of burning hung in the air. Only a shadow where Lavel had knelt to the Queen remained, scorched on the floor.

Morgaine turned to the peasant and his wife. They were shaking with fear. 'Did my son drink well?' she asked in the most condescending of tones. She glared at Mordred and at the empty glasses. 'I see that it is so. I must . . .' She searched for a phrase. '*L'addition*. I must pay the bill.'

The peasant's wife searched the air for him with her fingers. Morgaine frowned and advanced on the woman.

'Get away from her, you witch!' shouted Pat, but at a gesture from Morgaine, the words froze in his throat.

For an instant the Queen pressed the palm of her hand to Elizabeth's forehead. She smiled, glanced back at Pat and swept out of the lounge, followed by her son.

Elizabeth clamped her hand to her eyes and started to cry out. Pat clutched her tightly, rocking her in his arms.

She wept, screwing up her eyes because she could not bear or dare to look at the light that exploded against her senses.

'I can see. Oh my God, Patrick. I can see!'

Chapter 4

The Knight Commander spread his forces like a net to make a broad sweep across the woodland. But the main group he flanked along the length of the road.

Reports from his men muttered in his helmet as they advanced. The umberere screen in his visor threw up maps of their positions and pinpointed the placings of the enemy.

A scout group had reached the ground overlooking the lake. They relayed enhanced images of activity among the soldiers on the bank.

As was honourable before combat, the commander considered a challenge, but the Queen had herself presented such a credence to Merlin the previous night. Swords had been crossed, gauntlets exchanged. War had been declared.

Amongst the distant figures illuminated across his visor-relay, he recognised the errant traitor Ancelyn ap Gwalchmai: a Knight General deserter already stripped of his office, skulking amongst the enemy.

The commander vowed that his sword would answer this treachery with Ancelyn's blood.

There was movement beside the lake. An ugly beetle-shaped carriage was scuttling away from the encampment.

The commander called his men-at-arms into readiness and set them to spring the trap.

'See you at the hotel,' shouted the Doctor.

Winifred Bambera watched Peter Warmsly's packed car setting off along the road. Warmsly was in the back seat with the two young women. Lethbridge-Stewart was driving with the Doctor firmly ensconced in the passenger seat.

Since Lethbridge-Stewart had decided that all civilians should be cleared from the exclusion zone, it became increasingly apparent to Bambera that this exercise was not going to be a shared command. But when she looked from the old Brigadier to the Doctor, she could not decide which one was really in charge.

'They could have waited,' she muttered in her annoyance, half to Ancelyn, more than half to herself. She had favoured a convoy party with Major Husak to bring up the rear. One solid bolt through whatever was lurking in the woods.

Husak had been sent on ahead with more instructions from Lethbridge-Stewart.

Bambera shouldered her automatic rifle with resignation. 'Come on, Ancelyn. Looks like we get the deckchair.'

She climbed into the driving seat of Shou Yuing's 2CV and opened the other door for the knight.

'Let's hope there's enough methane in this old crock,' she said, as she searched for the keys.

They were not in the lock. 'Oh, shame!'

She heard jingling beside her and saw Ancelyn holding up a set of car keys for her.

'Do you seek these?' he said merrily. 'The Brigadier bid me give them to you.'

'I'm a brigadier too,' she said and took the keys.

He sighed to himself. 'These Old Times are not easily endured.'

'What?' said Bambera.

'Old legends that return to find us. I have Merlin and Arthur. You have your Lethbridge-Stewart.'

'Do you think we live up to their expectations?' she said.

He grinned. 'Do they live up to ours?'

She smiled back at him. 'At least mine isn't family!'

The old crock started first time and purred smoothly away from the lake.

'Winifred isn't following,' said Ace from the back seat.

'Good Lord, is that her name?' said Brigadier Lethbridge-Stewart.

There was a cold silence, which the Doctor took to mean: I wasn't talking to you!

Peter Warmsly sat silently, clutching the sword Excalibur in his hands, still dreading the moment when he might eventually wake up and find that all this was true.

'We may run into trouble,' said the Doctor cheerfully.

'Really, Doctor?' said the Brigadier. 'You surprise me. At least it looks as though Husak got through all right.'

'Brigadier Bambera'll be along in a moment,' the Doctor added. 'Probably just having another tiff with Ancelyn.'

'A tiff?' asked Shou Yuing. 'What, you mean like . . .?'

'Not while they're on duty,' interrupted the Doctor. 'Besides which, he's a perfick gentil knight.'

Ace shook her head. 'Winifred and Ivanhoe. Struth!'

They drove on for another minute and were just passing the parked TARDIS when the Doctor said, 'There's something wrong.'

'What?' they chorused.

'We haven't been attacked yet.'

Something exploded directly in front of the Range Rover.

Earth showered down on the windscreen as the Brigadier swerved violently through the smoke. The car mounted the verge and missed the fresh crater in the road by half a metre.

The Brigadier pressed hard on the accelerator.

'Everyone down!' he ordered and they slouched as deep into their seats as possible.

A row of men-at-arms blocked the road, their handguns raised against the oncoming vehicle. Beside them, the Knight Commander lifted his sword.

'Fire!' he yelled.

Lethbridge-Stewart swerved the Range Rover into a fish-tail. The skid caught three of the men-at-arms and knocked them into the bracken.

The car swerved clear off the road as the Brigadier skilfully changed the gear and trod on the accelerator again.

He was aware of the air exploding with fire and smoke around

118

them. He saw an opening in the trees, looked through the gap and took the car the same way, bouncing and jolting along a rough path, leaving their attackers in disarray.

'That surprised them,' he chuckled. In the rear view mirror, he saw the glint of their armour as they ran to and fro in confusion.

'Good car, Warmsly,' he shouted above the din.

The back window imploded, showering them in safety glass. The clatter of the blown-off rear bumper receded into the distance. They swerved a corner out of reach and were immediately back on the road.

The Brigadier reached for his personal radio. 'Greyhound One to Seabird. Are you reading me? Over.'

Bambera's voice crackled into the car. 'Roger Greyhound One. What is your message? Over?'

'Hostiles on the road, Bambera. Knights in armour. Lots of them . . . with heavy firearms. If you can't find another route, take them quickly. Over.'

'I copy you Greyhound One. Will act accordingly. Seabird out.' The line cut out.

'Who were they?' said Peter.

'What about my car!' said Shou Yuing.

The Brigadier ignored them. 'Now Doctor, happy?'

'Yes.'

'Oh, good.'

The Doctor straightened his hat. 'While Morgaine has people shooting at us, she won't be using more obscure methods of attack.'

'Such as?' said Lethbridge-Stewart.

'I don't know and I don't want to find out.'

Morgaine searched the white depths of her crystal for news. The air in the abandoned priory was still, but she felt disturbance, unbalance in the natural state. The glass was fogged. She caught only the frantic voice of her Knight Commander issuing garbled and desperate orders to his men.

The car, for that was how Françoise Eloise named the misshapen tin chariot, the car had eluded them. Morgaine had been foolish to expect a group of simple soldiers to waylay Merlin's plans. They had followed instructions; their honour was not besmirched.

Mordred watched her as she pondered her next move. Even in response he had his father's irritating manner. But Arthur had become a coward if he now sent Merlin out to fight his battles.

'The Knight Commander will stop them,' said Mordred.

'Stop Merlin,' she sneered. 'No, I shall deal with Merlin in my own manner.'

If Merlin was on the move, then the weapon, symbol of Arthur's power, was moving also. She would seize it soon enough. There was some devious plan hatching here, but she could not discern its purpose as yet.

Instead there were ways and weaknesses she would exploit. Icy water finds the crevice in the stoutest stone, freezes and splits it asunder.

Before her, etched into the floor, lay the octogrammaton of power. She stepped between the globes of ancient light into the heart of the pattern.

The bridge to her world was sealed, but energy still seeped across the abyss. She charged herself with its power. Her magic grew in might.

Before her, the glass cleared. She beheld another car travelling along the woodland road.

Shou Yuing's old crock moved surprisingly fast. Bambera knew nothing about the Chinese girl's brother, but she was impressed nevertheless. She thought all 2CVs had manual gear boxes.

She had already given up trying to persuade Ancelyn to put on his seat belt. 'You're from an alternative dimension, right?' she said.

'Yes.'

'Good, thought so. And you don't have cars there?'

'No.'

'Good, thought so. Hold on to the wheel and keep your foot on that.'

Bambera planted his hands firmly on the steering wheel. Reaching up, she pulled back the car's striped fabric roof.

She emerged into the air and clicked back the bolt on her AUG rifle. A change of barrel had converted it into an efficient light machine gun. She had four clear plastic magazines left: 120 rounds.

There was one lurch as Ancelyn struggled to drive at right angles a machine he had never seen before. Then he steadied and took its measure.

This guy is no idiot, thought Bambera.

She saw a flash of metal in the trees. Three men-at-arms burst from cover and started firing.

Bambera reckoned that Ancelyn's unfamiliarity with any vehicle at all, actually helped as they swerved along the road like a dodgem car. Or was it deliberate?

She returned fire in short deliberate bursts.

Sparks flew. The steady pap-pap of the men-at-arms' guns was no match for Bambera's fast delivery. The soldiers fell back into the woods.

'Foot down!' yelled Bambera and the little car tore past their bewildered enemies. The Brigadier threw back her head and let the wind tear at her.

'Magnificent!' shouted the Knight Commander as she passed. He watched her go as he relayed orders to the ambush that lay ahead.

'I still can't see them,' Ace called down to the Doctor.

The Range Rover was parked on the grass verge with Ace perching on its roof. She was surveying the road behind them with heavy duty binoculars.

'What about the bad guys?' called Shou Yuing.

'Them neither.'

Lethbridge-Stewart stabbed at the buttons on his radio and got no response. 'What's Bambera playing at?' he muttered.

'I don't like this at all,' said the Doctor.

The Brigadier straightened up. 'Don't worry, Doctor, Bambera is a highly competent and experienced officer. I gather the war correspondents book their flights for wherever she's going.'

'Oh, very reassuring, Brigadier.'

'She'll make it through.'

The Doctor grimaced as if he had a mouthful of something particularly unpleasant. 'War is a destroyer. It makes mockery of competence and experience.'

He tapped the Brigadier's radio and it crackled into life.

'This is Seabird. Piece of cake, Greyhound One. Will be with you shortly. Over.'

'Much relieved to hear it, Seabird. Over and out.' The Brigadier allowed himself the smallest ration of smugness with his smile.

'Professor.' Ace's voice came urgently from the roof. 'There's a whole pile of tinheads setting up on the road back there.'

The Doctor strained to see in the distance. He grappled for Lethbridge-Stewart's radio. 'Brigadier, tell Bambera she's in trouble.'

Winifred Bambera sat back behind the steering wheel and grinned. 'So tell me, Ancelyn. Are you married or what?'

'My lady is very forward!' he laughed. He turned in his seat to study her with his knowing blue eyes.

She spun a corner and saw rows of armoured soldiers blocking the road.

With a yell, she wrenched the wheel round. The car skidded towards a ditch. The men-at-arms opened fire in a blaze of flame.

A giant ball of flame rose above the woods. A moment later they heard the blast. Shou Yuing turned and buried her head in Peter Warmsly's anorak. He held her gently.

The Doctor stared grimly along the road at the distant billowing smoke.

Ace made to get back into the Range Rover. 'We've got to help them!' she shouted.

The Brigadier pocketed his radio. He showed no emotion. 'There's nothing we can do. The area's swarming with Morgaine's troops.'

She saw the Doctor trying to avoid her stare.

'Doctor?'

Her mentor shook his head.

'We'd better get back to the hotel,' said the Brigadier quietly. He turned and saw the look of unconcealed hatred on Ace's face.

Chapter 5

The rest of the journey back to the Gore Crow was completed in explosive silence.

The hotel drive was a mass of military vehicles. Soldiers were unloading weaponry and ammunition. Military hardware was being serviced. It reminded Ace of the activity she had seen around Coal Hill School in 1963. But here the weapons were sleeker and more nastily fascinating.

Major Husak, a heavy-featured Czech, came to meet them. He looked flustered and carried a clipboard. 'I'm glad to see you got through, sir,' he said as he saluted. 'Just a couple more names and I can get the evacuation completed.'

The Brigadier, his face grave, took Husak's arm and led him aside.

By the hotel's front porch, Pat and Elizabeth Rowlinson were standing like lost war refugees with a suitcase and several bags.

Peter Warmsly still clutched Excalibur in his arms. 'What's going on?' he said to the Doctor. 'Surely they're not turfing out Pat and Liz. They can come and stay with me.'

'I don't think so, Peter,' said the Doctor. 'They're clearing the whole area. You may well find yourself going with them.'

'Like hell I will.' Peter strode off towards his friends with the sword still under his arm.

The Doctor sighed and plunged his hand deep into a pocket. He produced a rusty tin whistle. Putting it to his lips, he gave a hearty blast that no one in the immediate vicinity even acknowledged. But K9 would have heard, he thought proudly.

Major Husak, his face tightly emotionless, approached the Rowlinsons and indicated a small minibus across the parking area. 'This way please, sir.'

Elizabeth stooped to pick up a bag and the Major bent in to help her.

'No, thank you,' she said curtly.

Husak stood back in astonishment as Elizabeth picked up the bag and walked towards the minibus.

Pat watched her go. There was a strong independence in her walk which made him want to cry, if only to weep with confusion. 'I apologize, Major,' he said curtly, his voice filled with barely concealed rage. 'You see, half an hour ago my wife was blind.'

Peter caught up with them as they reached the minibus.

'They're not going to evacuate me,' he said. 'Not so they can trample all over Trust land. I'll . . .'

He suddenly noticed that Elizabeth was staring at him with a slow confused smile.

'Peter?' she said.

'Liz? What's the matter?'

She shook her head. 'A woman touched my face and now I can see. She killed a girl and touched my face . . . and now I can see.'

'In you get, love,' said Pat and helped her up the step. He turned to Peter and found the Doctor standing next to them.

Peter pushed Excalibur into the Doctor's arms. 'You'd better have this,' he said angrily.

'And I have a few questions I want answered,' added Pat.

Peter continued, 'I have absolutely no intention of being evacuated! Here is where I live.'

'You're angry,' said the Doctor, catching at the depths of Pat's eyes. 'And you want to leave,' he went on, turning his glance on Peter.

'No, we do not want to leave!' protested the archaeologist.

The Doctor looked straight ahead between his assailants. His

124

voice became at once gravelly, compelling and persuasively subdued. 'Of course you want to leave.'

He turned towards Pat and fixed the agreement with his eyes. All rancour drained from the landlord's mind.

'Of course we want to leave,' he intoned gently. He could not imagine why he had thought otherwise.

'I wouldn't stand for any nonsense if I were you,' the Doctor warned Peter.

'Look, Doctor,' he complained as he took in the compulsion of the grey, blue, brown, whatever they were, eyes. 'The situation is perfectly simple. We are very angry. And we want ...' For a second he wondered what on earth he was talking about.

Of course, the eyes were reminding him ...

'... we want to leave. Is that right, Pat?'

'Don't get in our way,' said Pat.

'I wouldn't dream of it,' said the Doctor politely.

Peter faltered for a moment. He looked confusedly at the Doctor. 'I can't leave without Cerberus,' he said.

'Is that all?' The Doctor set the whistle to his lips and blew hard again.

There was a distant bark and the huge wolfhound dashed across the lawn and nuzzled eagerly against its delighted master.

'You monster! How did you get out?' cried Peter indulgently.

'Off you go then,' said the Doctor to the hound and bundled the evacuees into the minibus.

The Brigadier had been watching with the astonished Major.

Husak pointed to his clipboard. 'At the risk of being totally baffled sir, I have one more evacuee on my list. A young Chinese girl. Her parents are waiting in the village.'

The Doctor glanced at Peter Warmsly's abandoned car and then around the car park. He looked the Czech officer in the eye and said, 'I think she's already gone, Major. Tell her parents she's making herself useful. Thank you very much.'

The Major turned away satisfied and gave the minibus the clearance to go.

'Nothing changes, does it, Doctor?' said Lethbridge-Stewart with a look of tempered approval.

125

The Doctor surveyed the organized chaos of the operation. 'You have enough weaponry here to fight an army,' he said.

'That's the general idea.'

'It's useless, Brigadier.'

Lethbridge-Stewart had dealt with the Doctor's moods before. 'Not this time, Doctor,' he said patiently.

He signalled to a soldier, who carried over an open ammunition box. Lifting up one of the polished rounds, he said, 'Armour piercing, solid core with a teflon coating. Go through a Dalek.'

The Doctor raised an eyebrow. 'A non-stick bullet? They make frying pans out of this stuff.'

'UNIT R & D has been busy, Doctor. High explosive rounds for Yeti and a very efficient semi-armoured piercing high explosion round for giant robots. We even have gold-tipped rounds for you know what.'

'No silver bullets?' asked the Doctor.

'Silver bullets?'

The Doctor headed towards the hotel. 'You never know,' he said.

Good Lord, thought Lethbridge-Stewart. Now what?

'Quartermaster Sergeant!' he bellowed at parade ground volume.

The Sergeant was with him on the double.

'Silver bullets,' said the Brigadier. 'Do we have any?'

Elizabeth Rowlinson stared through the minibus window. Colours and shapes she had forgotten over twenty-two years of darkness paraded before her eyes.

Movement had been instilled in her memory as a series of tiny frozen photographs that progressed with jerky grace like an animated film or flick book. Real life flowed seamlessly.

The day was dazzling. Light on the grass, shadows among the trees. Thousands of shadow shades of shifting colours. Straight, angled and tangled; hard and soft; faces and bodies; all part of a giant, glowing kaleidoscope.

At last, things made sense.

Dear Pat was looking tired and Peter had the sort of kind face

126

she had always envisaged. Cerberus dribbled.

Along the drive were dark rhododendrons, pale multi-greened dogwoods and two girls darting for cover. Elizabeth met the eyes of the English-looking girl and smiled. The other girl had long black hair, almond eyes and could only be Shou Yuing.

Pat squeezed Elizabeth's hand. He was looking the other way. She had seen something he had missed. Now she had her own secrets again, not just what she was told.

It was too much to take in. She closed her eyes.

'You can come out now. They've gone,' said Ace.

Shou Yuing emerged from the bushes and said, 'That was close. I nearly got evacuated.'

Ace grinned. 'You may wish you had.'

At the front of the hotel, a group of soldiers were unloading a long shape shrouded in tarpaulin. Ace and Shou Yuing slipped round to the back and got inside through the garden door.

As soon as he saw them, the Doctor stepped in front of a dark shape that lay on the lounge floor. Ace didn't notice that he looked thoughtful and was holding his hat the way people do at funerals.

She did notice that he was trying to hide something. 'What's that?' she said.

'A shadow,' he sighed. He looked at Shou Yuing. 'You shouldn't be here,' he said.

'I know. My parents'll kill me.'

He nodded. 'A slight exaggeration, I expect.'

'Professor,' said Ace, 'we think we've sussed out where the legend of King Arthur comes from.'

'Oh? Which Arthur's that?'

'How many are there?' she complained.

'There's the eighth-century chieftain stroke rabble-rouser. He united all the warring tribes against the invading Saxons. But he wasn't a real king. Who did you have in mind?'

'The one in the ship, of course.'

'Ah. Tell me about him, Ace.'

Lethbridge-Stewart walked into the lounge. 'I'm sorry, Miss . . . erm young lady, but the Doctor and I have important matters to discuss.'

Ace ignored him. 'We reckon that when Ancelyn's lot dumped the freeze-dried King here, they must have told the story to some of the locals.'

'But they couldn't cope with the more outré aspects,' added Shou Yuing.

'So they translated it into terms they could understand,' Ace went on. 'And old frozen chicken becomes the King of the Britons.'

The Doctor's eyes narrowed with concentration. 'So the real King Arthur becomes the real Real Arthur ...'

'Doctor ...' said Lethbridge-Stewart.

'No, Brigadier, this is important.'

The ancient sword lay beside its scabbard on the coffee table. Ace lifted the weapon. It was heavy again.

'And since this is Excalibur ...' she said.

The Doctor snapped his fingers in triumph. 'Then it must be the source of Arthur's power. Why didn't I think of that?'

Ace grinned at Shou Yuing. 'And so it's a vital control element of the spaceship under the lake.' She raised the sword vertically with both hands and plunged it down. 'It wasn't stuck in the stone. It was plugged in!'

'Yes, you could be right,' the Doctor enthused. 'That's the trouble with parallel worlds.'

'What?'

He shook his head. 'They're parallel.'

Ace held up the sword again. 'I bet Ancelyn knows ... knew.' She looked at the floor, embarrassed.

The Brigadier took his opportunity at last. 'Doctor, Major Husak has taken a detachment to recover the bodies of Brigadier Bambera and Ancelyn.'

'What good are their bodies?' snapped Ace. She felt the Doctor's hand on her shoulder.

'UNIT looks after its own, alive or dead.' The Brigadier looked down at the human shape that lay burnt against the floor. 'And I want these ashes buried with honour.'

Ace went cold. She hadn't realized what she was standing in the same room with.

128

'Sorry,' she said. She didn't seem to have done much right lately.

The Doctor stroked her chin with the back of his fingers. 'That was very clever, Ace, what you worked out with the sword.'

'It was Shou Yuing too.'

'Yes. But I can't think of everything at once.'

'Thanks, Professor.'

There was a blurt of sound as the Brigadier's radio came alive. 'Husak to Greyhound One. The Seabirds are still operational. I repeat, the Seabirds are still operational!'

Morgaine stood at the heart of the octogrammaton, a web of power surrounding her. At her feet, enfolded in her cloak, sat her son. The crystal sphere, window across the worlds, hovered before them in the dark air of the old priory. Images flickered within its shape.

'The Knight Commander has failed,' said Mordred.

'Be not so harsh in your judgements, my son. This is Merlin.'

'But he has Excalibur.'

'Patience,' whispered the Queen. 'We have forestalled Arthur's arising. Now we shall use more subtle arts against his fool conjuror.'

The grimoires and books of lore that she had studied since she was a novice spoke of the spirits that dwelt all around them. As her knowledge grew with her power, she learned to bind the spirits to her will. The trees and the waters. The fair and foul fiends that went by the names of their tasks: the Lightning, Winds and Mists; the Menders and the Healers; the Destroyer.

Brigadier Lethbridge-Stewart spread the map across the coffee table and pointed to the road leading from the lake.

'Husak found the car here. They'd obviously abandoned it, because he found Bambera's beret further into the woods.'

'Well, at least they're alive,' said the Doctor.

'Yes, but Husak reckoned they were heading back to the lake.'

'Towards the missile convoy?'

'That's where Bambera's unit is.'

The Doctor squinted at the map again. 'But if they lead

Morgaine's troops there ...'

'It's a fully armed nuclear missile,' said the Brigadier.

'Don't you have procedures for situations like this?' the Doctor snapped.

'The unit's already on a Broken Arrow alert.'

'Oh, very reassuring.'

'I gather the next scenario is known as Bent Spear. I'll have to check procedures.'

The Doctor finally lost his temper. 'If there's an accident, Brigadier ... We have to stop any engagement. Is there a helicopter available?'

To the Doctor's annoyance, the Brigadier smiled knowingly and said, 'Much better than that, Doctor.'

He walked smartly out of the lounge and through the hotel hall into the open air.

The Doctor followed and was brought up in his tracks by the familiar object that sat in the centre of the otherwise deserted car park.

'Bessie!' he exclaimed in astonished delight.

Ace and Shou Yuing were already staring at the bright yellow, open-top, antique roadster.

The Doctor sauntered around his old car, beaming with pleasure as he checked for rust and scratches.

'I knew how fond you were of it,' called the Brigadier, 'so when you last went off on your ... "travels", I had it put in mothballs.'

'Does it run on petrol or steam?' teased Ace.

The Doctor climbed into the driving seat and refamiliarized himself with the deceptively veteran controls that he had once souped up so lovingly.

'For that,' he said to Ace, 'you can stay here. Coming, Brigadier?'

'Oh, Professor!'

'Too bad, Ace. Besides which, things may get dangerous.' He held up something stubby and white and pencil shaped. 'I want you to have this.'

'It looks like a piece of chalk,' she said.

'It is.' He dabbed her on the nose with it. 'I got it from the dartboard. It'll protect you from Morgaine's sorcery.'

'A piece of chalk?'

He suddenly looked gravely serious. 'At the first sign of anything strange, draw a chalk circle. As perfect as you can make it.'

'What, like in Dennis Wheatley?'

'I expect so. Then you and Shou Yuing stand inside with Excalibur and the scabbard.'

'Right, Professor.'

'Trust me, Ace,' he said.

'I do.'

'Good. And whatever happens, neither of you step outside that circle until I return.'

Shou Yuing barely managed to stifle a grin until she saw that Ace was as serious as the Doctor.

There was a twitter of energy as the Doctor clamped a small device over the hub of the steering wheel. He turned a lever on the top between his fingers. 'Running up to speed,' he said. 'Ready, Brigadier? Just pray we're not too late.'

The engine whined in an ascending scale. Strapped into the passenger seat, Lethbridge-Stewart tensed himself as if preparing for blast-off.

Ace nudged Shou Yuing. 'Nought to sixty in twenty minutes!'

'As fast as that?' said her friend.

'Appearances are very deceiving,' smiled the Doctor. 'Don't lose Excalibur and stay in the circle!'

There was an explosion of sound. Bessie vanished behind a cloud of white steam and smoke. Staggering back, Ace caught a flash of yellow from far down the drive.

The Doctor's hat tumbled out of the smoke and landed at her feet. Where Bessie had stood, there were two burning skid marks in the gravel.

'Gordon Bennett!' suggested Ace.

Shou Yuing giggled with amazement. 'Wicked!' she said.

131

Chapter 6

The two men-at-arms moved silently through the woods. The scent had gone cold. The quarry was lying low. They edged slowly forward fearing an attack.

With a blood-curdling scream Ancelyn ap Gwalchmai, flaxen hair flying, burst from the thicket and fell upon them. He caught and despatched both the soldiers with one whirling slice of his sword.

'Ancelyn!' hissed Bambera as she dashed after him. 'Can't you do anything quietly? You'll have Morgaine's whole army down on us.'

Like hers, his clothes were blackened by smoke and singed by fire. 'Let them come,' he cried. 'Do you not know, I am the best knight in the world!'

Ancelyn's blood was up for the fight. Hell's beard, but the warrior maid had spirit too. She had pulled him from the wreck of the car and covered their escape from Morgaine's troops with her gun. She was a different breed from the wan damosels who simpered in the households at home, embroidering their dainty graph-tapestries or mooning over some idyllic romance.

Yet Ancelyn had seen many a lusty knight sink into a pool of lovesick moping for such pale hearthkeepers. Lohengrin Cygnblen had fallen to Ilza of Brabann; Arveragus of Bretonesse forsook the field of combat to write poetry all day to the Lady Dorigen of Lyonce; worst of all, Ancelyn's comrade at arms, the gallant Tristremon, his rival in the lists, was suddenly seen sporting the favours of Ancelyn's own sister, that auburn-haired glacier Ysoldar.

Ancelyn had seen him lurking spaniel-eyed beneath her oriel at midnight, and caught him picking a nosegay from the hydropothecary's physic garden.

Ancelyn shrugged off such courtly nonsense and devoted his time to training for the battle that he was destined to fight. He still maintained his armour himself and cleaned the barrel of his own gun. He would not be unmanned by any castlebound maiden.

Yet strangest to tell, he would be content to do no more than watch the movement of Winifred's eyelashes across her pool-dark eyes. No more than that.

'Ancelyn?' said Bambera.

'Yes, my lady,' he replied in a reverie.

'On this world we have a great and honourable tradition of tactical withdrawing.'

He suddenly heard the shouts of the hunters closing on their quarry. 'You wish to run?' he asked. 'There can be but thirty of them.'

Bambera grabbed at his jerkin and pulled him close. 'Ancelyn, if you don't start moving, I'll kill you myself!' She grasped his hand and started to run. 'Now come on!'

He ran downhill with her, not too swiftly, to allow her the illusion that she was leading him. 'Winifred?' he shouted.

'What?'

Behind them, the shouts of the hunters grew fiercer.

'Art thou betrothed?'

She cursed. 'Not now, Ancelyn!' But her grip on his hand grew tighter.

Through the trees, they saw the glint of water. The convoy was closer than they had thought. Bambera let go of Ancelyn's hand.

Guards shouted as they emerged from the trees. Zbrigniev threw down the foam cup of tea he was holding.

They started to run. 'Get down,' yelled Bambera. 'Get under cover!'

Behind them, the woodland exploded in flame.

In the weightless crystal sphere, patterns of light were refracted
through space by spells of revelation. In their focus, they showed
a yellow carriage that sped along a sunlit trackway.

'You fool, Merlin,' muttered Morgaine, 'to place such a trust
with children.'

The patterns within the sphere shifted and revealed the room
of the hostelry where she had found Mordred. The two girls
were there, and with them, like a beacon in Morgaine's mind,
was the sword Excalibur.

'I swear that you shall rue this day . . .' She stepped from
the octogrammaton and threw up her arms in a gesture of power.
'. . . if you live!'

She was alone. She had sent away her son with specific
instructions. He had gone, eager to please, eager for a final
meeting with his sworn enemy, the traitor Ancelyn ap
Gwalchmai.

She took only moments to prepare herself, to quieten and
concentrate her mind. Steeped in the study of lore, the conjuring
of spirits came as easily to her as breathing.

As was her custom, she had partaken of no food or water
for that only weakened her as the vessel through which her
magic must flow.

In a normal summoning, she no longer needed the complex
rituals that other magicians relied upon, but there were still
spirits in the darkness that even she must fight to control: the
manifestations of total power in essence. Such demons must be
bound close to obey their summoners' will. They cheated and
lied in their struggle for release. And their forces could rebound
on the wizards who sought to use them.

In her hands, Morgaine held the silver chains with which she
would bind the darkest power of all.

And with that power she would destroy Merlin for ever.

A column of raw energy began to grow from the sphere within
the octogrammaton.

'With this fire I shall summon thee.'

Before its radiance, all the shadows in the priory seemed to

134

scuttle across the surfaces of the walls. Whispering like dead leaves, they gathered and sought refuge within the long shadow cast like a pall behind the Queen.

The shadow grew.

'With this silver I shall bind thee.'

The chains were gone from her hands.

Darkness slithered across the sky above the rafter beams. A cold wind blew against Morgaine's cloak and hair. She had opened the gate of hell and a foul, chill draught issued forth.

Somewhere cruel hidden eyes were watching her, but the demon could not resist her summons.

She heard the great breathing and the thud of its cloven feet. She turned and saw her massive shadow rearing up the wall. The silhouette had a life and shape of its own. It towered grotesquely above her, black as the pit of despair. And on its great shadowy head, there clustered a crown of curling horns.

'What did the Doctor say?' said Shou Yuing. ' ''At the first sign of something strange ...'' '

Everything in the past two days had been strange; so strange and so fast that she hadn't had time to draw breath and think. 'Strange' had suddenly become 'normal'; so how would she know?

Outside the deserted hotel, the daylight flickered. Above the empty bar, a hand-scrawled sign was pinned. *Under New Management*.

Ace pulled open an ammunition case and held up one of the silver bullets. 'Looks like Colonel Blimp has a fancy taste in hardware.'

'You don't like him much, do you?' said Shou Yuing.

Ace rested the bullet upright on the bar. 'I like being treated as a person. Not a ''latest one''. Anyway, I don't trust him to guard the Professor's back. That's my job.'

She flipped the Doctor's hat up her arm and on to her head the way she'd seen him do it. 'And if he really is Merlin ... You know what that makes me, don't you?'

Shou Yuing giggled and shook her head.

Ace lifted Excalibur and held it out like a wand. 'The

sorcerer's apprentice,' she cried.

Inside and outside, the light dimmed noticeably.

'Do you think that counts as strange?' said Shou Yuing. Her voice had taken on a fresh tremor of fear.

Ace fumbled in her jacket pockets for the chalk.

They dragged the furniture to one side and pulled up the carpet. Behind the bar, Shou Yuing found a length of string. They attached it to the chalk.

It was getting too dark to see. The sky had turned to a threatening bronze that seemed to suck away the light. Shou Yuing held one end of the string to the stone floor, while Ace circled her slowly with the chalk. It took three attempts to produce something approaching a perfect continuous circle.

Standing together in the centre, with the sword and scabbard between them, they watched the darkened room beyond the circle.

'Do you think we should sprinkle holy water or something?' said Ace.

'I don't know,' Shou Yuing said. 'I'm Chinese. It's not my mythology.'

Ace lit a candle she had found. She sorted through the dozen packets of crisps she had lifted from the bar as supplies. 'What flavour do you want?' she asked.

'But it's the middle of the afternoon, isn't it?'

Ace swallowed hard. 'It was the last time I looked.'

'Then why is it so dark?'

It was a bizarre sensation, decided the Brigadier. On the few occasions when he had driven Bessie, the car's superdrive facility had always been removed by the Doctor, forcing him to stay within the speed limit. Now, as the Doctor opened the superdrive up, the countryside became a blur that flowed smoothly past with unreal velocity.

The speedometer indicated only thirty mph, which was ludicrous until the Brigadier realized that the needle was going round for the second time.

He glanced behind them and saw a sudden darkness growing like a thundercloud above the land towards Carbury. Ahead

136

there was black smoke rising.

As they topped Bedivere's ridge, Bessie's wheels locked and she skidded to an abrupt halt. The Brigadier threw out a hand to steady himself, but the veteran roadster's drive system neatly absorbed all inertia. Its passengers, one of whom expected to be hurled through the windscreen and halfway along the bonnet, were left safely ensconced in their seats.

The Doctor stood up and stared over the top of the windscreen.

'I think we're too late, Brigadier,' he said grimly. He climbed out of the car and gazed down the hill in fascination.

There was battle by the lake. Explosions and gunfire through the drifting smoke. He heard men shouting, screaming and dying.

The Doctor was already angry with himself. He had felt the strength of Morgaine's power and knew her forces would not be confined to human soldiers for long. Soon she would summon darker powers. The chalk he had give Ace might be the correct response to any attack that Morgaine unleashed, but it was also exactly what Merlin would have done.

Every way he turned, however much he tried to resist, the answer was always the same. He might as well have scrawled THE DOCTOR WAS HERE all over the walls of the spaceship. Ace could show him how.

He had been set up by the future. Merlin was behind all this and he, the Doctor, was destined to be Merlin. It was unavoidable. One day, barring accidents, he would travel into the past of another universe and trigger the events he had forced himself to endure now.

He took out the spare hat that he always kept in his pocket and planted it on his head. He felt no better.

Merlin had put Arthur into suspended animation for some reason; perhaps the High King himself would explain when he awoke. But he might not take kindly to being woken, only to find that this was not the hour of England's greatest need.

The Doctor looked at his watch . . . just in case.

At all costs, Morgaine must be prevented from reaching Arthur first, for she certainly meant him some harm. There was enough damage being done already.

And her men must be prevented from laying hands on the nuclear missile. The Doctor trusted no one, not even himself, with such an infernal device. It was irresponsible in the extreme to leave it lying about like that. He was glad he had left Ace behind.

The UNIT vehicles had been pulled into a circle surrounding the missile launch vehicle. Morgaine's troops were subjecting them to a barrage of gunfire from all sides.

Further off, the Doctor could seem more men-at-arms emerging from the trees. The UNIT troops, for all their hi-tech weaponry, were vastly outnumbered.

To his surprise, he saw several figures breaking away from the cluster of vehicles. The man leading them had a mass of yellow hair and must be Ancelyn. Beside him was another figure in UNIT fatigues and wielding a sword. It was Winifred Bambera.

Men-at-arms, immune to the bullets, were running to meet them in hand-to-hand combat.

Fools, thought the Doctor, for neither of them was wearing armour. 'What good will any of it do?' he said aloud.

'I sometimes wonder myself,' said the Brigadier who was standing next to him.

The Doctor turned back to the car. 'Come on.'

'Doctor, I've just received the most peculiar message from the hotel.'

'What? Did it say anything about Ace and Shou Yuing?'

The Brigadier climbed into his seat. 'No. All they said was "Night has fallen here." '

The Doctor looked back towards the darkening sky. He thought for a second.

There was a fresh barrage of explosions from the battle. They had started using grenades.

'I'll deal with the hotel later.' He started Bessie's engine. 'First I have to stop this bloodshed.'

'How, Doctor?' said the Brigadier. 'Stand in the middle and shout?'

The Doctor looked at him in surprise. 'Good idea,' he said.

138

Bambera searched for Ancelyn through the fighting. She saw him once from a distance, tackling two men-at-arms, but then she was set upon herself.

Her men were dying and she loathed it. She had followed Ancelyn out into the open, because he was the only one who understood their way of fighting and she had to learn it too.

She was trained in fencing, but a broadsword was another matter. Ancelyn said she was a born warrior. He told her to watch her footwork and let the force come after the blow.

When they saw she had a sword, they lowered their guns. But even then they seemed reluctant to attack her. She suspected it wasn't honourable to take on a woman. But it was them or her, so it was them. So much for honour.

Killing and maiming with a gun was surgical in comparison. First it had been smoke. Now it was blood. They both sickened her. The sword hilt bit into her bare hands. But she was desperate to find Ancelyn; and desperate for her soldiers to survive.

How did she stop it? Kill their leader? Capture their standard? The fighting had moved away from her and was concentrated on the convoy again. Through the explosions, she heard Ancelyn's voice shouting for Mordred to come and meet him.

Then the shouts stopped.

She stumbled over the top of a ridge and saw the enemies facing each other, ten metres between them.

'Mordred,' called Ancelyn. 'Face me, Mordred. Is your army not enough to give you courage?'

'Courage?' the Prince sneered. 'To face you, Ancelyn, who fled the field at Camlaan? Ancelyn the Craven, I call you.'

Bambera ran down the slope to Ancelyn's side. 'Forget about being noble, Ancelyn. Get under cover!'

Ancelyn grinned at her and stood his ground. 'What care I for the words of a half-man, who cowers from a woman's wrath.'

They raised their swords in fierce salute. Winifred stepped back as the two men, screaming all their hatred, charged towards each other.

From nowhere, another figure darted between them.

Flinging his arms wide, the Doctor yelled, 'Stop! I command it!'

Whether by a trick of his own or by some natural acoustic, his voice carried across the entire field of battle. The fighting stopped. The smoke drifted and cleared. The armies turned to a man and stared as the figure mounted the ridge. He circled, addressing men-at-arms and UNIT troops alike. He did not shout, he simply said with quiet authority, 'There will be no battle here.'

The soldiers waited. They looked around them, bewildered at the dead and injured. They knew, as he had learned, that Merlin stood amongst them once again. A single voice cried out in pain and then was silent.

One sound alone disturbed the battlefield. Mordred was laughing.

'This is not a battle,' he said. 'It is but a ruse. A diversion.'

It was like a thunderclap. The Doctor slowly walked down the ridge towards the prince. 'No,' he said, but he knew that he was wrong.

Morgaine, whom he had never met, knew him of old. She knew his mind and his weaknesses.

Mordred smirked. He pointed to the dark sky. 'My mother hath summoned the Destroyer. The Lord of Darkness, Eater of Worlds. Look to your child guardians, Merlin, for soon they shall be no more.'

He bowed low and walked away.

'Ace,' whispered the Doctor. 'What have I done?'

Beyond the pool of candlelight there was nothing.

Ace held the sword, Shou Yuing held the scabbard. They sat back to back in the centre of the circle, staring at the chalk line that held back the unnatural light.

They might have been adrift in the void.

Shou Yuing tapped the seconds out on the floor with the scabbard. It was annoying Ace.

'So your grandparents run a takeaway in the village.'

'Yes,' said Shou Yuing.

'I could murder chow mein and noodles.'

140

'They do pizza.'

'Yeah?'

Shou Yuing went on tapping. The crisps were untouched. The candle flame guttered with a hiss.

'What did you say?' said Shou Yuing.

Ace shifted position uneasily. 'What?'

'I thought . . . Nothing.'

Someone's getting jumpy, thought Ace. She shivered. She wanted the Doctor back now.

Tap, tap, tap.

There was nothing to do and nothing to say. She was suddenly angry.

'This is stupid,' she complained.

'What did you call me?' snapped Shou Yuing.

'I said "this is stupid",' articulated Ace, loudly. 'You deaf or something?'

'No, you didn't! I heard you. You called me stupid.'

Ace got to her feet and stood over Shou Yuing. 'I am not a freak!'

'What you getting jumpy for?' said the Chinese girl.

'I said I'm not a freak, right! I'm Ace. You dumb or what?'

Shou Yuing clambered to her feet, scattering crisp packets across the circle. 'I am not stupid!'

'Then why do you say stupid things?'

They were eye to eye.

Shou Yuing's face tightened with hatred. 'That's good coming from a misfit like you!'

Ace started to back slowly away. 'You watch your mouth, toadface! Or I'll knock your teeth in!'

'I bet nobody likes you,' Shou Yuing went on.

'Shut up!' shouted Ace. She felt the darkness pressing around her.

Shou Yuing was leaning closer. 'First chance he got, the Doctor went off without you.'

'Shut up! Shut up!'

'I bet even your parents hated your guts!'

Ace saw red. 'Shut up you yellow slant-eyed . . .'

She froze. The back of her neck was tingling. She was on

141

the very edge of the chalk.

Shou Yuing was slowly edging backwards.

Ace tumbled forward and they clung to each other at the centre pool of light.

'Someone's playing games with our minds,' whispered Ace.

The darkness beyond was not as dark as they had imagined. Something was moving there.

'Avallion breeds her children strong,' said the woman outside the circle. She was tall and frighteningly beautiful with hair like a cascade of fire. Her armour glinted in the light of their candle.

'No matter. There shall be an end to these games.'

She stretched her slender fingers and gazed longingly into the circle. Shou Yuing and Ace shrank from her smile. Ace grabbed the sword and scabbard from the floor.

Then the woman spoke again, the threat was absolute. 'I am Morgaine of the Faye. I am power beyond your imaginings.' She stretched an open hand towards them. 'Surrender to me what is mine by right of conquest. Give me Excalibur.'

Ace clutched the sword tightly. 'Never.'

In the shadows behind the woman, a darkness was rising. They heard the clink of chains and the deep breathing of a monstrous beast.

'Then you shall be given over to the Destroyer ...'

It came like a summoned dog, standing in Morgaine's wake, swaying slowly, its great form devouring light. Its breath came in rasping growls and a stench of warm corruption.

'... and be his handmaidens in hell.'

Part 4

Scenario: Nukeflash

*. . . when all else fails, duck. It's not practical,
but it can be momentarily comforting.*
UNIT Procedures Manual,
Zen Division.

Chapter 1

It lies with you, my son. Do not be snared by Merlin's wiles. We must have Excalibur.

In his head, Mordred heard his mother's instructions. At last, in her moment of greatest need, she placed a trust with her son. His confidence grew bolder before the Wizard's threats.

'Tell Morgaine to call off the Destroyer,' demanded Merlin.

Mordred shouldered his sword and met Merlin's glare with mockery. 'Surrender to our justice and the children will live.'

With a flourish, Merlin hooked the red curled device at the end of his wand over Mordred's sword. He tugged the blade hard against the Prince's neck.

'Your justice?' he snarled 'Tell her to call it off, or I'll decapitate you!'

Mordred could not move. Again, his mother's voice cut into his thoughts.

Fear not, my son. It is all deceit.

He was encouraged, even with death biting at his throat. 'We know you of old, Merlin. You would not kill.'

The blade did not relent. 'I wouldn't count on it.' Merlin's eyes burned with the same fury that Mordred remembered from a different face an age ago.

'Come then,' challenged the prince, 'look me in the eye and end my life.'

Merlin's look blazed. His teeth clenched as he steeled himself for the deed. The blade nicked at Mordred's skin.

Then with a look of despair, mighty wizard Merlin flung the sword away and stood back.

Mordred smirked at his defeated foe. 'It is a weakness, this lack of spirit.'

He had rewarded his mother's trust and shown that he was no coward. At last, he would share in every appurtenance of her triumph.

Cold metal suddenly pressed against his head. An old warrior clutched at his shoulder.

'Try me,' said the soldier and Mordred heard the priming click of a primitive gun.

Ware this man, Mordred. He is steeped in blood.

'Brigadier,' complained Merlin, 'this is not the way.'

'I'm sorry, Doctor.' The soldier was unperturbed. 'Can Morgaine hear me?' he said to the prince.

'Yes.'

He raised his voice to issue demands. 'Listen to me, Morgaine. Leave my world or your son dies.'

Mordred waited for his mother's reassurance. Moments passed. There was no new thought in his mind. He felt blood trickle on his neck. Why did she wait?

'Deathless Morgaine. Save me!'

She would release him. She would find some other means to win the accursed weapon.

Finally her cold thoughts came.

Die well, my son.

'Mother!'

Morgaine's troops had regrouped along the ridge beside the dig. Their leader came to attention as the Battle Queen's orders issued from his helmet.

Knight Commander. Recommence your attack. Take no prisoners.

The commander saluted. Strategy options scripted out on the inside of his visor, instantly relaying to his company of men-at-arms.

'We shall make honour our standard. Put down your guns.

145

Draw your swords. Let good steel be our conscience.'

To a man, the soldiers raised their weapons in salute to their mistress and their enemy.

'Do them honour. Kill them all!'

With one cry, Morgaine's army descended upon the remnants of the UNIT forces.

Bambera was first to see the tide of soldiers bearing down on them. She yelled a warning to Lethbridge-Stewart.

He pushed Mordred ahead of him. 'We'll try the direct approach, Doctor.'

'Agreed, Brigadier.'

'Bambera, we may be able to put a stop to this at source. You're in charge here.'

Freed of the gun's threat, Mordred scoffed, 'You are as weak as Merlin.'

'I take that as a compliment,' said the Brigadier, and he pushed the Prince towards Bessie.

Bambera turned to direct her men and found the Doctor beside her. He seemed unconcerned by the advancing army.

'Winifred, they mustn't take control of the missile.'

The first shots were being fired.

'Leave it to us, Doctor.'

He smiled and walked directly through the line of fire towards his car.

'My mother will destroy you,' Mordred was saying.

The Brigadier pushed him onto Bessie's back seat. 'Frankly Mordred, I'm getting a little tired of hearing about your mother.'

'Hold tight,' said the Doctor as he climbed into his seat.

The sonic burst of the car's overdrive drowned the explosions from the battlefield. To the south, the sky over Carbury was thick with darkness.

Bambera hefted her Styer AUG in her hands. As a machine gun, it had a maximum range of 2600 metres, but armour piercing rounds were useless against Morgaine's soldiers. Even at twenty metres, the bullets just ricocheted off.

Grenades were making some inroad into the attackers, but

explosives were wrong for an enemy who killed with such respect for their adversaries. It was boiling down to hand-to-hand combat again.

It was no surprise to find Ancelyn beside her.

'This is our part, to fight and die,' he said, his eagerness tainted full of grim laughter.

Amid the screams of death, she understood. Their lives were the barricade that shielded others. Death had to be laughed at.

She clasped his arm. 'That's what we're paid for.' Throwing down her gun, she lifted a sword. 'So let's do it with some style.'

His eyes gloried in it. She felt sick. Together they ran into battle.

The yellow car hurtled along the country lane.

'Your friends will soon be dead,' said Morgaine.

The vision faded from the crystal globe. She pushed the sphere away. It coursed through the air and vanished into the huge horned shadow that loomed over the room.

Ace and Shou Yuing crouched together in the circle, dreading each contemptuous glance from the sorceress.

'Now,' said Morgaine, turning her full attention upon them, 'give me Excalibur.'

Clutching the sword tightly, Ace got to her feet. 'If you're so powerful, why don't you take it?'

A deep growl emanated from the shadow.

Morgaine raised her hand to strike the insolent brat. But she was blocked. The flesh of her palms whitened and flattened against a wall of invisible force that held back her anger.

Ace did not move.

Morgaine's arms began to shake. The harder she pressed, the more her hands became like claws. Finally, she snatched them back in disgust.

'The sword is protecting you,' she said.

Ace raised Excalibur. 'The Doctor was right. You can't touch us while we're in the circle. Not while we've got the tin-opener.'

The Battle Queen remained remarkably composed. There was no panic, which frightened Ace.

'This is true,' said Morgaine. 'I cannot break such an enchantment.'

147

'But I can,' said a deep, dark voice.

Out of the great shadow stepped a figure. A man of aristocratic bearing, impeccably attired in a twentieth-century business suit. He was handsome; so handsome, he was almost ugly. Every beautiful feature on his face was slightly exaggerated, like a near-perfect mask, to conceal something very terrible beneath. His skin had a metallic blue sheen. He moved with a casual, predatory grace and was over seven feet tall. Behind him, the horned shadow traced his every movement.

'I am the Destroyer,' he said by way of introduction, but his voice rasped with a barely controlled snarl. 'I could obliterate you.'

Ace held the sword tightly to her. The Doctor had been right in every respect so far. Excalibur might still protect them. 'If you're so bad, why haven't you done anything?'

For a moment, she caught the malevolent glint of a jewelled reptilan eye. She shuddered. Shou Yuing clung to her leg in fright.

'First I must be freed. This immortal has me chained.' The Destroyer lifted his arms to show Ace the manacles that bound him. His eye pleaded, *use your sword*.

'You are bound with silver,' warned Morgaine.

'It burns,' intoned the humanoid monster.

'Good,' she smiled.

Ace was startled. In the hallway through the door, she saw movement. There were soldiers with guns out there. The squaddies left behind to guard the building. They were taking up positions to attack.

The Destroyer had turned back to Ace. He nodded towards Morgaine. 'She fears me,' he confided.

'I fear nothing,' protested the Queen.

'Then free me and let me claim this world!'

'Perhaps,' she said.

The soldiers outside were getting ready to move.

'What does he want the world for?' Ace called quickly.

There was a deafening burst of gunfire as the soldiers sprang into action.

The Destroyer was distracted by a spray of bullets that tore into his chest. He looked at Morgaine.

148

'Kill them,' she instructed.

He threw out an elegantly manicured hand and emerald light burst from his fingers.

Ace flung herself over Shou Yuing as protection from the blast. The room outside the circle became an inferno of blazing green fire.

When it cleared, the soldiers were gone. Smoking shadows lingered, scorched on the floor and walls.

Ace looked up, terrified. Shou Yuing was shaking.

The Destroyer straightened his tie. 'What do I want with your world?' He bared his pointed teeth and drooled down his jacket. 'Why, to devour it. What else?'

He tugged at the chains on his wrists.

Morgaine paced slowly around the circle until she faced her demonic servant. She pointed to Ace and Shou Yuing. 'Get me that sword,' she commanded.

Bessie skidded to a halt in front of the hotel.

Smoke was drifting from the doorway. Windows had been shattered. Green light flickered inside.

The Doctor climbed from the car and poked at the gravel with his umbrella. A funnel mark of soot across the drive marked out the blast from inside the hotel. There was a smell the Doctor recognized only too well as that of burnt human flesh.

'My future is catching up with me,' he muttered for no one's benefit in particular. He looked up at Mordred, who was still under the Brigadier's supervision.

'This is the Destroyer's work,' said the Prince grimly.

There was a thunderous roar and a blast of green energy erupted from the porch. It hurled the Brigadier and Mordred to the ground. The Doctor stood silhouetted, his arm shielding his face from the fierce light.

Then it was gone.

He lowered his smoking sleeve and yelled, 'Morgaine! If they're dead ...'

He ran headlong through the smoking entrance.

Before the Brigadier could catch him, Mordred was up and running away down the drive.

149

Decisions, decisions. For a moment, Lethbridge-Stewart was torn between who to follow. But he had to know what was happening, if only for the report he would have to write.

He found the Doctor standing amid the rubble and matchwood that had been the hotel lounge. He was holding a small earring in his hand.

'Ace. Shou Yuing,' he said quietly. His face was grey with guilt. His hat, his first hat, lay in the dust. He took off the replacement, furled it up and pocketed it. Then he scooped up the original, brushed it off and wearily placed it on his head.

'I'm sorry, Doctor,' said the Brigadier. 'We should ... '

'Is that you, Professor?' said a muffled voice.

A pile of debris shifted and fell apart. At the bottom of it, beneath the coffee table that had sheltered them, crouched Shou Yuing and Ace. They were covered in soot and plaster dust.

'Ace!' the Doctor exclaimed. 'And Little Cloud too. Thank goodness. What happened?'

'The hotel fell on us,' complained Shou Yuing, not overtly impressed by the Doctor's linguistic prowess.

'And there was this woman with a pet demon,' added Ace.

'Morgaine and the Destroyer,' agreed the Doctor.

Ace levelled with him. 'And I also remember a chalk circle that was supposed to protect us.'

'You're still alive, aren't you?' he complained. 'Where's Excalibur?'

'Ah,' said Ace.

Shou Yuing looked awkward and said quickly, 'The woman seemed to want it very badly.'

'Very, very badly,' concurred Ace.

'So we gave it to her,' Shou Yuing added.

'Good,' said the Doctor.

'I mean, it's not our fault,' Ace protested. 'Now if I'd had some nitro ...' She faltered. 'What do you mean, good?'

The Doctor shrugged. 'Oh, just that exotic alien swords are easy to come by.' He dabbed a smudge from her nose with his scarf. 'And Aces are rare. Have you got the scabbard?'

Ace brimmed with something like love for him. She held up the battered relic.

'Well, that's something anyway,' he said.

'Doctor,' called the Brigadier. 'What do you make of this?'

Across the lounge by the fireplace, the air was shimmering like a heat haze. The Doctor scrutinized the miasma for a moment.

'How did Morgaine leave?' he asked.

'Big flash of light and gone,' said Ace.

The Doctor picked up the scabbard and tentatively extended it towards the heat haze. There was a crack of static and the air ahead opened up like a tunnel of swirling light.

'That's where she went,' said the Doctor. 'Through an interstitial vortex.'

'So now what?' said Ace.

He lowered his head thoughtfully and looked at her under the brim of his hat. 'Excalibur seems to be the crucial element in all this. We have to get it back from Morgaine.'

'She's dangerous, Doctor,' interrupted the Brigadier. 'And as I recall, interstitial transfer involves a lot of technological nonsense. Machines.'

The Doctor grinned. 'Brigadier, you remember.'

'The Master with a Greek accent? I'd been trying to forget.'

'Greek!' said the Doctor. 'You should hear his French one! But Morgaine doesn't use machines. She has the Destroyer.'

Ace was getting bored with all this 'old boy' back-slapping. 'Professor,' she complained, 'why don't we just nip through the vortex and jump the witch?'

The Doctor looked suddenly grave. 'Passing unshielded through this vortex would be insanely dangerous. The forces loose inside could rip you into molecules, if you're lucky.'

There was a moment's silence.

'Shall I go first?' asked the Brigadier.

'No, me,' insisted the Doctor. 'Ace?'

'Stay here,' she said. 'Yeah, yeah . . .'

The Doctor tidied his jacket, straightened his scarf and pulled his hat on tight. 'High drama is just the same as comedy, Ace. It's all a matter of timing.'

He and the Brigadier stepped into the swirl of the vortex together and were gone.

Chapter 2

'Where is my army?' demanded Morgaine.

The Destroyer raised his head and savoured the air. His groomed hair was turning coarse. From his temples, two small nodules were starting to break through the blue-grey skin.

'Your army has gone the way of all flesh,' he growled with relish.

Smoke drifted across the silent battlefield, an insubstantial veil that failed to obscure the horrors it might have hidden.

Warriors from two universes lay bleeding in the muddy grass. Many were dead. UNIT soldiers and Morgaine's troops. Medics moved among them, searching for the living.

Ancelyn sat on the ground, wiping the blade of his sword with a bit of rag.

Beside him, Winifred Bambera dabbed at a gash that had cut through her sleeve into her arm. The missile was secure, but there were reports to make and casualties to deal with.

A body in full armour lay twisted in front of her where it had fallen. She knelt and pushed open the visor. The dead eyes of the Knight Commander stared coldly up at her. The officer could be hardly more than sixteen years old. Ancelyn's sword had punctured his breastplate. But the Commander had attacked first . . .

'A good fight,' said Ancelyn.

Anger boiled up in Bambera — her usual reaction. In all her

life, she had never been able to cry. Ancelyn, she prayed, might teach her.

The strange, flaxen-haired knight gently touched the wound on her arm.

'My lady?'

'I told you not ... Oh, never mind.'

Shou Yuing squinted into the turmoil of the vortex tunnel. Its two dimensional surface stretched impossibly into infinity just in front of the fireplace. A wafer-thin illusion that had swallowed the Doctor and Brigadier whole.

'They're going to be killed,' she said to Ace. 'You saw what the Destroyer could do.'

Ace had been turning over the wreckage of the bar. 'Morgaine could control the Destroyer. She had it chained up. With silver chains. Get it?'

'The silver bullets,' exclaimed Shou Yuing. 'I thought that was for werewolves.' She glanced back to the vortex. Darkness was starting to flicker in its deeper regions. 'Ace, I think it's starting to fade.'

'Got them.' Ace reached under an overturned armchair and extracted the case of silver bullets.

'It's going,' warned the Chinese girl.

Ace moved back to get a clear run at the vortex.

'Are you going to throw them through?' Shou Yuing said.

'Do me a favour,' said Ace. She ran like a bowler at the flaring crease in time/space.

'Geronimo!' The vortex wrapped around her and closed up like a slammed door.

Shou Yuing stood on her own. She was only a bystander in the game and now the action had moved elsewhere. She wondered if she should wait in case another demon turned up and needed sorting out. Shou Yuing and the Monkey King. She hadn't stopped to think until now; she wasn't sure she wanted to think. Monsters and knights and soldiers. Her car was written off and people were dead. Suddenly she wanted to go home and have a good row with her parents.

A storm of darkness loomed above the priory.

Morgaine watched the Destroyer as it did her work. It struggled against her adjuration, as she knew it would. In the real world, where her power was stronger, the demon would be helpless. In Avallion, every struggle it gave loosened its mask a little more. Its glittering reptile eyes sought a means of release. They never left her as it worked out her orders. The Beast beneath its visage was laughing. Its human features soured and twisted. Its close curling horns reached outward. It was strong and growing stronger.

The sword Excalibur rested on its point at the centre of the octogrammaton, held in a tapestry of spells that the demon wove around it. The globes of ancient light at its sides flickered once more with energy drawn from another universe.

Almost complete. Then only she, Morgaine, could touch the weapon. And Arthur would be powerless.

The Destroyer, its breath coming in hot hungry gusts, turned towards her. 'You would do well to release me, Morgaine.'

'Release you?' she said contemptuously.

'Merlin is mighty and cunning. I cannot destroy him while I am chained.'

'And let you run havoc? No. I have Excalibur. Merlin cannot touch me ere I am gone from here. See. The gateway is almost complete.'

The Destroyer's blackened lips twisted into a grin. 'He comes even as we speak.'

'How? He cannot come through the vortex . . .' Suddenly she knew that the fiend, even bound to her, played with her fate as its toy. 'You have allowed him access . . . Why?'

But she knew the answer too well.

'So that you will be forced to release me.'

And if she lost control over the demon, she would be the first that it carried off. She tested her will against the monster, it was still her slave. Its trickery waxed stronger, but she could turn an advantage from that as well.

In the corner of the derelict hall, the air wavered and opened like a flower of swirling energy. Out of its heart stepped the Doctor and the Brigadier.

'Morgaine,' said the Doctor, raising his hat.

The Brigadier instinctively raised his pistol and released a volley of rounds at the looming menace of the Destroyer.

The demon snarled and looked down with irritation at the bulletholes in its suit.

'Brigadier!' snapped the Doctor.

Lethbridge-Stewart sniffed dimissively. 'Nothing ventured, Doctor.'

'Nothing gained,' growled the demon. It flung a taloned fist into the air in a gesture that lifted the Brigadier from the ground and tossed him like a discarded doll through the rotting wood of the wall.

'That was uncalled for,' yelled the Doctor.

He made a run for Excalibur, his hand ignoring the spells in which the sword was bound.

Morgaine's hand reached the hilt first. She snatched the sword to her and met his eyes across the power web of the octogrammaton.

'Your move, Merlin,' she sneered.

Merlin and Morgaine. Ancient immortal enemies as the tales tell. Their battle joined once more.

The Doctor held up his umbrella like a sword. But when Morgaine raised Excalibur to parry his attack, he simply slid his brolly teasingly along the length of the sword. It cut the material to ribbons, but it enraged the Battle Queen into the bargain.

'You haven't won the game yet,' he declared.

He slowly began to circle the octogrammaton, forcing her round to maintain her opposition.

'I could always defeat you at chess, Merlin,' she warned.

He stopped, for Morgaine now had her back to the open portal of the vortex. Behind him, he heard the Destroyer laughing to itself.

'Who said anything about playing chess?' said the Doctor. 'I'm playing poker!'

Ace hurtled out of the vortex with a whoosh and collided with the Queen. The sword flew from her grasp, spinning through the air until its hilt dropped homeward into its maker's open hand.

'And I had an Ace up my sleeve,' he cried, brandishing Excalibur.

The vortex slammed shut.

'Very funny,' complained Ace as she scrambled to her feet.

Morgaine turned in rage to the demon. 'Destroy him!' she yelled.

The creature stepped forward and raised its chained arms. 'Release me.'

Its demand was too eager. Morgaine's actions faltered.

'Which is it to be, Morgaine?' goaded the Doctor. 'Who do you fear more?'

'This is no threat, Merlin,' she cried. 'Return Excalibur or I shall unleash the Destroyer upon this world.'

'Stuff and nonsense,' snapped the Doctor.

Morgaine's eyes blazed. She turned upon the demon and flung wide her arms in a gesture of release.

The links of wrought silver fell apart and the manacles splintered. With a smile that grew from a snarl to a roar, the Destroyer raised its hands in triumph.

Its shape altered and grew. The tailored suit split as great thorns spiked out across its body like the armour of all Hell's legions.

Its head lost all human features; its skin hardened into scales of metallic blue; its goat horns twisted and blackened in thick murderous spires. As it rose up, its eyes narrowed and darkened into green pits of burning evil.

Ace clung to the Doctor. 'Nice work,' she said.

He stared up at the towering abomination. 'I thought she was bluffing,' he said lamely.

The Brigadier lay in the long grass outside the priory wall where he had been thrown. His head was awash with disparate thoughts and memories ... or were they just his fancy?

Doris was patting down the soil around the apple tree.

On Radio 4, the newsreader was saying:

The General Secretary of the United Nations Intelligence Task--force, Mrs Eva Carlshorst, has again denied reports of casualties amongst UNIT personnel operating in the south-west of England ....

Doris was reaching for the portable phone.

'I want to speak to Brigadier Alastair Lethbridge-Stewart.' Her hair caught the sunlight through the french windows and glistened. 'Well, where is he?'

A gloved hand seized the Brigadier's collar and yanked him up into reality.

Mordred's face was barely inches from his own.

'Where is she?' he demanded.

The Brigadier swallowed wearily. 'To whom are you referring?'

The Prince swore and pushed him back to the ground, before stalking angrily towards the priory door.

'Free!' roared the Destroyer. 'Free!'

The demon slavered as its brutal frame grew still more immense; its arms raised, already pressing against the skeletal beams of the roof. It gave off a stench of putrefaction.

'You fool, Morgaine,' accused the Doctor. 'Do you think this'll solve anything?'

He stepped back in awe of the monster, and before he knew it, Morgaine had again snatched Excalibur from his hands.

Holding the weapon against her enemy, she backed within the bounds of the octogrammaton. 'Too late, Merlin. The gateway is open. I am gone and you are lost!'

She turned to leave, but the door of the hall was flung wide open. On the threshold stood Prince Mordred, his sword in hand.

'Mother!' he said.

'Mordred.' Again she faltered, confronted by the child she had herself sacrificed.

'And about time,' complained the Doctor.

'You live,' said Morgaine, her voice trembling.

He advanced into the hall, ignoring the monster that loomed above them all. 'No thanks to you, false parent! Witch!'

'Mordred, I thought you were dead.'

'Thought or wished it so?'

He stepped into the octogrammaton with her and she raised a hand to stroke his hair. 'Mordred, no. That was not the way of it.'

As they started to fade, the Doctor swung out with his umbrella handle and hooked Excalibur away from Morgaine. She turned with a glare of helpless rage. Then she and her son were gone.

Morgaine's legacy loomed over the Doctor and Ace. The Destroyer, waiting, taking great draughts of air, as a dragonfly rests after its emergence, before launching on its first flight.

The Doctor was staring up at the monstrosity, intoxicated by its manifestation of raw evil. Of the 7,405,926 demons on the Talmudic table, this fiend probably made it into what Ace would call the Top Ten.

Ace tugged at his sleeve. 'Doctor, can I have a word ...' She hardly dared move for fear of attracting the demon's attention.

The Doctor took her arm and they edged for the door.

'Merlin ...' The Destroyer's voice came deeply and slowly.

The door opened and Lethbridge-Stewart barred the way. His eyes widened as he took in the towering presence of the Destroyer. He met its cold glare and knew he was a marked man.

'Brigadier, you're going the wrong way!' The Doctor grabbed his shoulder and tried to force him back. Behind them, the monster began to stir.

Ace fumbled in her pockets and panicked. She looked back and saw her case of bullets lying on the hall floor, near the Destroyer's taloned hooves.

She ran back.

'Ace!' yelled the Doctor.

As she grabbed up the case, the monster's hoof kicked out wildly and took her on the hip. She went tumbling across the hall, only to be caught somehow in the Doctor's arms.

He hurried her out, followed by the Brigadier. As they ran into the evening air, they heard the Destroyer's cry of rage and hunger.

The Doctor found a path that led away from the building. Once they were clear of the priory grounds, he set Ace down. She was only winded and sat quietly recovering her breath.

There was a steady distant rumble like growing thunder. The shell of the priory was beginning to flicker with green light.

'What was that?' said the Brigadier.

The reply was almost casual. 'That, Brigadier, was the end of the world.'

The old soldier nodded. 'Same as ever, eh Doctor?' But he had not forgotten the predatory eyes or how they had damned his soul.

The Doctor stamped at the ground with his brolly. 'Oh, this is no good at all!'

'I can have an airstrike in minutes,' suggested the Brigadier.

'No. Conventional weapons won't even scratch it.'

'How about silver bullets?' said Ace.

'Silver would do the trick, getting some is another matter.'

'Professor.' She held up the bullet-case for him.

The Brigadier finally appreciated the care with which the Doctor selected his relentlessly unorthodox companions. 'Splendid,' he said.

The Doctor beamed at the contents of the case. 'Excellent work, Ace. Brigadier, give me your gun.'

He opened the pistol and started to load the silver rounds into the chamber.

'You er ... just fire the bullets into the monster, do you?' enquired the Brigadier.

'Yes, yes, it's that simple, like most killings.' The Doctor snapped the gun shut.

'Good Lord,' said the Brigadier, staring over the Doctor's shoulder. 'Look at that spaceship.'

'What?' As the Doctor turned to look, he was caught square on the jaw by Lethbridge-Stewart's fist.

He went down senseless.

'You toerag!' Ace stared in blind rage as the Brigadier picked up the pistol.

'Sorry Doctor, but I think I'm more expendable than you are.'

He ran back down the path towards the burning priory, leaving Ace alone, furiously trying to rouse her mentor.

Along the path he ran, his feet pounding and his breath short. But he had to face those cruel eyes again.

Doris was on the phone and getting angrier.

'Yes, I am Mrs Lethbridge-Stewart ... A message? Oh, I don't know. Tell him I lo ... Tell him he hasn't finished the garden.'

Their apple tree, full grown, heavy with russet fruit; then a great wind tore at it, ripping its roots until it crashed in ruin across her lawn.

Alastair Gordon Lethbridge-Stewart reached the door of the priory. The ground trembled. Smoke was curling acridly into his lungs as he pushed his way inside.

Timbers and rafters blazed around the Destroyer like a throne of green fire. It was hunger. This world was its to devour, and then another and another. All life would not assuage the terrible famine that raged inside its heart. Its raised hands belched energy, out through the burning roof into the sky.

It exalted in its freedom and roared its agony. Hunger would prevail. 'And today I shall feed!'

Beside its hooves, it noticed the figure of a human. With a convulsive movement, it drew its power back into itself and fixed him with its eyes. It knew him.

'Little man, what do you want?'

The Brigadier levelled his pistol at the demon. 'Get off my world,' he said.

The Destroyer bared its fangs. 'Pitiful. Can this world do no better than you as a champion?'

'Probably,' said the Brigadier and unleashed every round he had in the gun.

Tiny impact explosions flared on the demon's armoured hide. The monster began to laugh. A laugh that sounded the death knell of all creation.

The Brigadier lowered the gun in defeat. 'I just do the best I can,' he said.

The Destroyer stopped laughing.

Light flared from the bulletholes in its chest like lasers through the smoke. The glare spread and burst out, flaring into a vast, cold green sun.

The blast caught the Doctor and Ace as they belted down the priory path. They kept running.

The building evaporated in a surge of energy that tore skywards.

'No chance,' yelled Ace as they ran.

Amongst the discarded burning rubble, they saw the blackened body of the Brigadier.

The Doctor knelt by him in anguish. 'You stupid, stubborn, thick-headed, numbskull . . .! You were supposed to die in bed! I could've handled it myself. It wasn't your job!'

Ace kept quiet. It was the first time she had seen the Doctor weeping.

'Rubbish, Doctor,' said the Brigadier, opening his eyes.

'You're supposed to be dead,' complained the Doctor.

'Sorry to upset the eulogy, but you don't really think I'm so stupid as to stay inside ... do you?'

'Well ...' The Doctor was laughing now.

'Really Doctor, have a little faith.' He looked at his friend's embarrassed companion. 'Ace?'

'Yes, Brigadier,' she smiled.

'I'm getting too old for this. From now on, he's all yours.' He clambered awkwardly to his feet. 'I'm going home to Doris as soon as possible.'

The Doctor looked startled and delighted. 'So, she finally got you,' he grinned impishly.

'Yes,' laughed the Brigadier. 'I suppose there'll be clearing up to do first. There usually is with you, Doctor.'

'Just a small nuclear missile bogged down in a nature reserve.'

The air had begun to clear. The smoke dispersed into the crystal blue sky.

'What about this?' asked Ace. She lifted up the sword Excalibur.

The Doctor frowned. 'That old thing. What do you make the time, Brigadier?'

Lethbridge-Stewart consulted his precious gold watch. 'Eight minutes to six.'

'Ace?'

She looked at her plastic-strapped, underwater, tune-playing, digital display, computer game kilowatch. 'I don't know about here, Professor. On Iceworld it's twenty past seventeen. Why?'

The Doctor lifted his own *horloge de main*, a unique timepiece given to him by Beaumarchais for a couple of one liners in *The Marriage of Figaro*, to his ear. 'According to this, it could finally be the hour of England's greatest need.'

Chapter 3

Ancelyn stepped through the portal into the darkened ship, his eyes wide with wonder. 'This is the long-lost Dromond of the High King.'

It was the same sense of wonder, the Doctor decided, that explorers experienced at the discovery of every archaeological site from Telos to the Valley of the Kings. Seals were broken, dust was disturbed and heaven knows what was unleashed.

Ace and the Brigadier exchanged glances as the young knight launched into a tour guide spiel: 'Lord Merlin grew this mighty ship in a great embryo vat for Arthur's final campaign . . .'

'Yes, yes, Ancelyn,' said the Doctor, 'but there are more important matters to attend to. Don't imagine that Morgaine will give up so easily.'

'Is that why we're going to wake up old uncle Arthur then?' said Ace.

'Just gather round,' complained the Doctor. 'This isn't a school outing.'

He led the way towards the bier at the far end of the hall. A single shaft of water-dappled light fell across the recumbent shape of the High King encased in dusty armour.

He was relieved that Ancelyn did not actually fall to his knees at the sight of the sleeping monarch. They each simply took up places around the obsidian slab.

The Doctor took his hat off.

'Now Ancelyn, replace Excalibur and King Arthur will arise.'

Ancelyn smiled gravely and passed the sword. 'I think the honour belongs to the Brigadier,' he said.

'No, the Doctor should do it,' Lethbridge-Stewart blustered.

Ancelyn was persistent. 'No my lord, you were the victor.'

'Give me that,' said Ace. She took the sword from the knight and planted it back in the stone.

'Ace, have you no sense of ceremony?' complained the Doctor.

'No,' she said.

Immediately the lights came up.

The ribbed arches of the great ship, covered in veins like scrollwork, lifted out of darkness for the first time in centuries. Coloured screens like tapestries. Panels slipped open on a vast window of murky green water. Everything lay under a grey snow of dust. There was a sound of deep movement in the walls.

'Listen,' cried Ancelyn. 'She is alive.'

The King did not stir.

They waited.

'This is very odd,' said the Doctor eventually.

'You put him here,' said Ace.

'I "will" put him there.'

He reached out and touched the helmet. A trickle of dust slipped out from behind the visor. There was rust on his fingers.

'What is it, Professor?'

The Doctor pulled the helmet away from the body. Apart from dust, it was empty.

'Good Lord,' said the Brigadier.

'Where is the King?' asked Ancelyn.

Ace caught at a brown piece of parchment that tumbled with the dust from the helmet. It had a thin spidery script in what looked like ancient felt tip.

'This is for you, Professor,' she said.

He looked uncomfortable. 'What does it say?'

The parchment was so brittle it started to crumble in her hands. 'Dear Doctor, King died in final battle, everything else propaganda.'

'Who signed it?'

'Mine sincerely, the Doctor.'

Bother, thought the Doctor. 'I'm sorry, Ancelyn. The present rarely lives up to expectations.'

They stood silently for a moment, the Doctor moved by the death of a friend he had yet to encounter. 'And who's going to tell Morgaine?' he said.

Ancelyn looked startled. 'I have left my lady Winifred unguarded.'

He bowed to them and ran from the hall.

The Doctor looked at his other old warrior friend. 'I could have given myself a bit more warning. You two can see to this ship.'

'Explosives, Ace?' asked the Brigadier.

'Now you're talking,' she said.

The Doctor turned to go. 'We'll give Arthur a warrior's burial.'

Brigadier Bambera sat in the temporary comfort of her Command Vehicle. She tugged at the fresh field dressing on her arm. Others of her unit had been less lucky. Eight dead, seventeen injured. It was what Ancelyn called 'a good fight'.

She tapped her pen irritably on her desk, but the right words to start her report eluded her. There was a rig on the way to move the missile at last. And they were having trouble keeping the press away.

But what preyed on her mind most was wondering how long Ancelyn would stay. She put down her pen and yelled to Zbrigniev for more coffee.

There was no answer.

She got out of her chair and walked to the door. It was too quiet outside. She came down the steps and rounded the side of the trailer.

Zbrigniev was lying face down in the mud. There was blood on his jacket.

Before Bambera could react, a sword was pushed against her throat.

'The battle's not done yet,' whispered Mordred in her ear.

A figure, tall and cloaked in gold with long flame-coloured

hair, stepped into Bambera's vision. 'I am Morgaine the Deathless,' she said. 'I have need of your engine of war.'

Morgaine mounted the Command Vehicle steps and her son followed with their prisoner.

Inside, the knowledge of Françoise Eloise was enough for the Queen to reason which bank of the ugly controls she required.

She manipulated the primitive instruments, searching with her mind into the machine's logical junctions and magical procedures. Easy as a child adept's sleight of hand.

Within one minute, a screen printed out its display. *Sagamore Missile Prelaunch Sequence Complete. — Enter Fail-safe Release Code.*

This was the first wall. Françoise Eloise knew no more. Morgaine turned with a gracious smile to the warrior maid.

'This engine needs particular instruction to make it live.'

Bambera, held tight in Mordred's grip, glared contemptuously. 'It's a nuclear missile. The blast will kill you as well.'

'Oh, we shall be long gone ere that happens. Now tell me, what is the secret incantation?'

'I don't know what you're talking about,' said Bambera.

'The magic words — the "Fail-safe Release Code".'

'No idea.'

'I doubt that,' said Morgaine. She leaned forward and stared into the tiresome creature's eyes. In this instance, she did not require a full mind. She only needed one slip of knowledge. 'What is the code?'

Bambera stuttered and her eyes rolled upwards.

Ancelyn knelt by the body of Winifred's sergeant-at-arms. This was the third corpse he had encountered on returning to the UNIT encampment.

It was an attack from within, for the stationed guards had no trouble to report.

The door to Winifred's command pavilion opened and Mordred stepped forth. He carried Winifred over his shoulder.

He flung the woman to the ground and she lay unmoving. Ancelyn gripped the sword and called the prince's name.

They faced each other at last. Ancelyn, a mortal without hope, could never take the life of his immortal enemy. His family had suffered through generations under the yoke of the tyrant queen and her bastard son; but such impediment was nothing now the life of his own beloved Winifred had been snatched.

With a roar, he flung himself upon Mordred. Sparks flew from the ringing steel. They clashed, locked by hatred into one final test of strength. Pushing against each other; their ferocity matched.

In a *coup de pied*, Mordred abandoned honourable combat. Twisting his foot around Ancelyn's ankle, he forced the knight backwards, stumbling into the mud.

Mordred raised his sword to finish the job, but a figure in eccentric dress darted between them. It casually threw out a hand that sent the astonished Prince toppling over.

'Excuse me,' said the Doctor as he hurried up the trailer steps.

Ancelyn was up in a moment. Steel clashed again as the enemies renewed their tournament.

Morgaine spun in her chair as the Doctor entered the Command Vehicle.

'Too late, Merlin,' she crooned.

The VDU screen that she sat before displayed a Countdown to Detonation symbol. It was flicked remorselessly from 74 to 73 to 72.

'Not when there's an off switch,' the Doctor said. He scanned the control bank and saw a recessed red button marked 'Abort' in Japanese.

She followed his glance and caught both one and then the other hand as he reached for the button.

'No,' she said and pushed him back.

He had not anticipated her strength. She matched his attack with ease.

'If this missile explodes, you will die,' he growled. 'Millions will die.'

'I shall die with honour, knowing that cursed Arthur dies with

166

me.'

'All over the world, fools are poised ready to let death fly,' he insisted. 'One spark will turn into an inferno.'

'What do I care — when Arthur is such a coward that he will not face me?' Her eyes were blazing with rage. 'This is war!'

'You hate Arthur so much?' he asked, trying to force a way to the console.

She forced him away again. 'I offered Arthur the greatest gift — the enduring power of the immortal. He snatched it and turned against me. For twelve centuries have I waited to destroy him.'

31 — 20 — 29 —

'And what else will you destroy?' Anger and pity mingled in the Doctor's voice. 'Folly from the sky. Blind. Random. No one is safe, no one is innocent. Machines of death, Morgaine. Who needs the Destroyer? A scream from the sky. Light, brighter than the sun. No war between armies or nations — just Death. Death gone mad!'

He felt a slight resistance in her strength and redoubled his attack.

17 — 16 —

'A child looks up at the sky. His eyes turn to cinders. He weeps ashes. Is this your honour? Is this war? Are these the weapons you would use?'

She could no longer face him. Her eyes were full of tears. 'Tell me!' he cried.

Her head shook. 'No,' mouthed her lips.

'Then stop it, Morgaine! End the madness!'

She released his hand and pressed the red button.

01.

Time froze. The Abyss receded a little.

The Doctor closed his eyes and breathed deeply.

Morgaine's eyes were cold as she issued her challenge.

'I honour your petition, Merlin. Now tell Arthur to meet me with honour in single combat. It's time he ceased hiding behind your coat-tails.'

The Doctor looked down at the countdown symbol. 'Arthur is dead,' he said quietly.

She was startled by his bluntness. 'No,' she smiled. 'I don't believe you.'

'It's all true.'

'Merlin, Prince of Deceit! This is another trick.'

'Arthur never took your immortal gift, Morgaine. He died over twelve centuries ago.'

'You lie . . .'

'You know better than that.'

'It cannot be.' She steadied herself on the control desk. Her voice submitted to the yearning so long submerged beneath the hatred that drove her.

'Arthur, who burned like starfire and was as beautiful. Where does he lie? I would look on him one last time.'

'He is gone to dust,' said the Doctor.

'Then I cannot even have that comfort.' The Battle Queen trembled and her will was lost. 'I shall never see him again. Arthur. We were together in the woods of Selladon . . . The air was like honey.'

'I'm sorry, Morgaine,' said the Doctor. 'It was over long ago.'

The sound of clashing swords outside had ceased. The Doctor extracted the computer abort key from the console, pocketed it and left Morgaine alone with her tears.

The battle between Ancelyn and Mordred had run its course. The knight was a better and more agile swordsman, but the Prince, with the advantage of his powered armour, tired less easily.

Ancelyn's responses were growing weary. His attack turned to the defensive. Finally, a mighty blow smashed the sword from the knight's blooded hand.

Ancelyn backed up against the trailer. The point of Mordred's sword pressed into his stomach.

'I do not fear death, Mordred,' he said. 'Your noble father, the High King, is dead also. I have seen his body.'

The Prince's eyes narrowed.

'Come, despatch,' Ancelyn demanded. 'You have slain my beloved. There is no life without her.'

'So be it,' said the Prince and pulled back the sword to strike.

The swing of a rifle butt knocked him senseless. He fell at Winifred Bambera's feet.

'Shame,' she said.

'My lady . . .'

She dropped the rifle and massaged her injured arm. 'Nice speech, Ancelyn. Next time check that I'm dead first.'

The door of the Command Vehicle opened and the Doctor stepped out.

'Ah Winifred,' he said quietly, 'I have a prisoner in here for you.'

'That makes two then,' said Bambera and she pointed to the unconscious Mordred.

The Doctor nodded inside the trailer. 'I don't know what you do with imprisoned royalty these days. I doubt the Tower will hold her, but treat her with honour anyway. She's just had a nasty shock.'

From the lake came the deep boom of an underwater detonation.

A second later, the surface erupted into a white column of solid water a hundred metres wide against the evening sky.

Along the promontory, the Doctor saw two figures. One, solid and stentorian, stood watching the explosion, unblanching at its fury. The other, tiny and nimble, capered around the first in a sort of dance of triumph.

The Doctor put his umbrella up. It was torn to shreds.

That night, it rained fish in Carbury.

Chapter 4

It was warm enough for Doris to show the Doctor around the garden. She had been wary of the stranger to begin with, but now their arms were linked and they laughed together like old friends.

'I'd wondered about a surprise reunion for Alastair,' she said. 'Or would he clam up at the thought?'

'I'm sure he'd secretly love it,' smiled the Doctor. He twirled his brolly, which had been refitted with camouflage disruptive pattern material, as he admired the daffodils.

'And you must come and bring anyone you'd like,' Doris went on. 'We've plenty of room. It's a shame you missed Easter.'

'Christmas,' the Doctor suggested. 'It'll give you time to prepare, and me time to fetch everyone. They're a bit scattered.'

She looked at him knowingly and squeezed his hand. 'Christmas which year, Doctor?'

'Ah, I see that Alastair trusts you,' he said.

'And I trust him, Doctor. Don't worry, he was very discreet.'

They rounded the rockery and saw the Brigadier seated on a garden swing chair beside the little apple tree. He was deep in conversation with Ancelyn.

'He's very charming, isn't he?' said Doris. 'But a bit intense. And I wish he'd take his sword off.'

The Knight stood up and bowed as they approached.

'Here I am, dear,' said Doris.

'Talking strategy again, Brigadier?' asked the Doctor.

Lethbridge-Stewart, relaxed and genial in a red cravat, looked a little perplexed. 'Yes, you could say that,' he said.

There was a shout from the house end of the garden. 'Ready,' yelled Ace. She waved and disappeared around the side.

Doris waved back. 'Coming.'

'Are you going somewhere?' said the Brigadier.

'Mm. Out,' said Doris.

'Out?'

'Out with the girls.' She laughed and headed towards the house.

The Brigadier shrugged and set off after her with Ancelyn and the Doctor in pursuit.

Bessie stood on the drive in front of the house, her yellow paintwork gleaming. On her back seat sat Shou Yuing and Winifred Bambera. Ace was at the steering wheel. They all wore old fashioned driving goggles.

'Ace,' accused the Doctor, 'I thought you said this was a piece of antiquated junk.' He looked nervously at what his protegée might do to his car.

'I found these in the glove compartment, Professor. Are they yours?'

She handed him an ancient and crumpled paper bag. It was full of rock-hard jelly babies.

'Mind how you go,' he said and quickly pocketed the bag.

'We'll try not to break too many speed records,' called Shou Yuing. She had skipped lectures to come for a long weekend from Exeter.

'Or traffic laws,' added Winifred. On her hand, she wore a crystal ring inlaid with twining silver leaves, emblem of the House of Garde-Joyeuse.

The Doctor noticed her meet Ancelyn's eyes for a second and then look away with a barely disguised smile.

Doris had put on her goggles and climbed into the passenger seat.

'Do you want to drive?' asked Ace.

'Oh no, dear. I'll drive on the way back.'

'Erm, how far are you planning to go, Doris?' asked the

Brigadier.

'You get busy with the garden, darling,' she said. 'The grass needs sorting out.'

'But what about supper?'

She was unperturbed. 'That's a good idea. Have something really nice ready for us.'

Ace started the engine. It exploded into life and then settled into a simmering purr.

'Wicked,' said Doris.

Ace put her foot down and Bessie scorched away along the drive.

Ancelyn gazed after them. 'Ah, Lord Merlin,' he said in awe. 'Are they not magnificent?'

Merlin again, thought the Doctor. He wondered how long he might stave off his inevitable destiny. There were so many possibilities. With luck he might spend several lifetimes avoiding it.

'Are you any good with a lawn mower, Ancelyn?' asked the Brigadier.

'My lord?'

'Round the side of the house. Go and see what you think.'

The Doctor resigned himself to his immediate fate. 'I'll make supper,' he said.

He watched the young knight disappear on his latest quest. The problem of Morgaine and Mordred remained, but that was not his burden. Their punishment was for Earth to negotiate with Ancelyn's home world — a different universe that he intended to avoid for as long as possible.

That place, deprived of its monarchy, would soon be a crucible of political ferment. The formal processes designed to choose a new crowned head would doubtless be relentlessly complicated and bound by codes of honour. They might run for years and lead to fresh battles.

Nothing so easy as a sword in a stone.

'I'm glad of a free moment, Doctor,' confided the Brigadier. 'You see I've just had a job offer it would be hard to turn down.